The JAZZ Method for SAXOPHONE

John O'Neill

*Dedicated to Betty O'Neill (1930–1990) who nurtured and shared my love of music,
and Ken O'Neill (1927–1991), who bought my first saxophone.*

SCHOTT
EDUCATIONAL
PUBLICATIONS

This is a very musical presentation of basic saxophone playing techniques, and since the whole reason for playing the saxophone—or any instrument—is to play the best music possible, I think this text offers a rare opportunity for a new player (or a more experienced one) to develop a really musical facility as he observes the basic procedures for making a good sound on the saxophone.

A welcome addition to the jazz improvising library.

Lee Konitz

ACKNOWLEDGEMENTS

Many of the ideas in this book were inspired by five great teachers: Don Rendell, who took me under his wing when I was just beginning, and continues to be a wise and generous friend and great source of encouragement; Peter Ind, who introduced me to the ideas of Lennie Tristano and told me to listen to Pat Metheny; Lee Konitz, with whom I had a very fruitful transatlantic tape-exchange, and who gave me a new direction and discipline for my improvisation; the late Warne Marsh, who gave me a lifetime's study in two lessons; and Larry Teal, whose book *The Art Of Saxophone Playing* helped me to resolve nearly all my technical problems in my formative years when I was struggling to teach myself.

I would also like to pay tribute to Lennie Tristano, the greatest jazz educator of them all. Although I did not study with him personally I am conscious of having absorbed many of his ideas through the teaching of Lee, Warne and Peter, three of his most celebrated students.

I would also like to thank the following people:

Phil Lee, Jeff Clyne and Paul Clarvis for their superb musicianship, professionalism, patience and creative contribution during the recording of the accompaniments. Special thanks to Phil for his many helpful suggestions concerning the harmony and arrangement of my music.

The staff at Schott & Co. Ltd for their encouragement and assistance.

All the composers who submitted work to me. There was much excellent material which I could not use. Special thanks to Ted Gioia and Tony Crowle.

All my students, who played such an important part in shaping the book.

Nick Taylor of Porcupine Studio for his engineering and mixing.

Henry Binns for his photographs.

John Minnion - whose drawings were even more accurate than his leg-spin bowling!

Thanks to Bob Glass of Ray's Jazz Shop for his help in compiling the discography.

Willie Garnett for looking after my instruments.

My family and friends, especially Sylvie, James, Sophie, Caroline and Robert, for their unwavering support and belief.

Jean Thomson for helping me find my way.

British Library Cataloguing-in-Publication Data. A catalogue record for this book is available from the British Library

ISBN 0 946535 20 5

© 1992 Schott & Co. Ltd, London
Reprinted 1993

CONTENTS

The publishers would like to thank the following for allowing the use of their material in this publication:
John Minnion for the illustrations.
Henry Binns for the technical photographs.
Steve Berry, Dave Cliff, Tony Crowle, Ted Gioia, Peter Hurt, Lee Konitz, Roland Perrin and Don Rendell for their compositions.
Bocu Music Ltd, Ecaroh Music Inc., Marada Music Ltd and Prestige Music Ltd for their copyright music.

The author and publishers also wish to acknowledge, with thanks, Redferns Music Picture Library/Photographers: David Redfern (Gerry Mulligan, p. 11; Sonny Rollins, p. 11; Benny Carter and Coleman Hawkins, p. 11; Stan Getz, p. 24; Miles Davis, p. 36; Louis Armstrong, p. 39; John Coltrane, p. 49; Count Basie Band, p. 59; Ben Webster, p. 66; Lee Konitz, p. 71; Gert Schlip (Sidney Bechet, p. 11), William Gottlieb (Thelonious Monk, p. 46; Lester Young, p. 55; Charlie Parker, p. 87), Bob Willoughby (Paul Desmond, p. 84). © Redferns, London

INTRODUCTION

To the saxophone player

My aims in writing this book were to give you a thorough grounding in basic saxophone technique; to develop good general musicianship and knowledge of music theory; to encourage you to find your own voice and creative powers; and to foster a love of this exciting heritage of jazz music, which in itself is a labour of love on the part of all the musicians who have contributed to it. These should also be your aims, and whatever difficulties you may encounter try not to lose sight of any of them.

An essential component of this method is that the foundation techniques of breathing, embouchure, tone production and tonguing are discussed in depth. Mastery of these techniques is the key to playing the saxophone well, and every aspiring saxophonist must tackle them **from the beginning** or risk acquiring bad habits which could take months or even years to rectify.

It is therefore essential that your enthusiasm to get on with playing the music does not lead you to overlook the first section of the book. You should feel comfortable with the exercises in Part One before you start Part Two.

This book also sets out to give you a systematic approach to learning to read music, covering the most common rhythms that a jazz musician is likely to encounter. There is a popular misconception that reading music is somehow not as relevant for the jazz musician, usually accompanied by the equally mistaken notion that jazz players play 'off the top of their heads', with little knowledge of music theory. This sometimes encourages beginners, already nervous about the prospect of reading music, to feel that they can dispense with this task.

Although it is true that jazz is primarily an oral tradition, music notation has become increasingly important as the music has grown in complexity, and is a vital means of preserving and communicating information. You should therefore regard the ability to read music competently as a prerequisite.

The early tunes have deliberately been kept as simple as possible so that you are able to develop a good basic sense of pulse and to become accustomed to the basic fingering positions before tackling the rhythmic complexities of jazz.

Each chapter introduces either a new note or notes, a specific technical or rhythmical problem, or a new concept. You should not depart from the order in which the chapters are set out. Many of the chapters finish with suggestions for further listening, reading or practice, and you are advised to adopt as many of these suggestions as possible in order to gain maximum benefit from the method.

The accompanying CD is integral to the method, and will add an extra dimension to the music. The early stages of learning to play a musical instrument, when you have not yet acquired the skill to play with other musicians, can sometimes be frustrating, and the CD is designed to 'keep you company' in what can otherwise feel like rather a solitary activity, and to give you practice in the discipline of group-playing. Eventually you will be able to join a group or form your own and to enjoy the social aspect of making music with other people. If your speakers are connected properly the accompaniment will be heard from the left speaker and the saxophone from the right speaker. By using the 'balance' controls on your music system you will therefore be able to adjust the 'mix' between saxophone and accompaniment, or indeed to filter the saxophone out completely. This means you can choose to play with or without the saxophone for guidance. There are also several pieces which give you the further option of playing a duet part.

If you find that any of the music on the CD is too fast then practise slowly, perhaps using a metronome, and gradually build up to playing with the accompaniment.

There is often more than one way of understanding or solving a particular problem.

The important thing is to keep an open mind and never to believe that you have learnt all there is to know about any aspect of playing music!

This book is not a rigid 'classical' method. Once you have learnt to play what is written you should feel free to alter rhythms, embellish or improvise. Many of the tunes will benefit from being treated in this way.

Above all ENJOY YOURSELF!

ABOUT THE SAXOPHONE

The saxophone was invented in the early 1840s by Adolphe Sax, a Belgian instrument maker who was experimenting with the idea of fitting a reed mouthpiece to a brass instrument. The resultant hybrid soon found favour in marching bands as an instrument which combined the flexibility of the woodwind family with the carrying power of the brass.

The saxophone has never really established itself as a permanent member of the orchestra although an impressive list of composers have written for it, including Bartók, Berg, Bernstein, Britten, Copland, Gershwin, Hindemith, Kodály, Milhaud, Penderecki, Prokofiev, Rachmaninov, Ravel, Schoenberg, Shostakovich, Strauss, Vaughan Williams, Villa-Lobos, Webern and Weill.

However, it is in the jazz world that the saxophone has achieved its greatest popularity, particularly since the 1930s and the advent of the great big bands, where the instrument's power and versatility was used to great effect by arrangers like Fletcher Henderson, Count Basie and Duke Ellington. It was during this period that the first great soloists like Coleman Hawkins and Lester Young began to emerge, and the potential of the saxophone to express tremendous individual differences in tone-quality began to be appreciated.

There are many different types of saxophone, but the four in most common use are soprano, alto, tenor and baritone. All of the saxophones are fingered in exactly the same way, but they are pitched in different keys–the soprano and tenor in B♭ and the alto and baritone in E♭. This book can be used by players of both B♭ and E♭ saxophones, provided you have the appropriate version of the CD accompaniment.

The soprano is the hardest saxophone to play in tune, while the baritone is a considerable weight. Beginners therefore usually start on the alto or tenor. If you are unable to decide which saxophone to play you should listen to as many different examples of the different saxophones as possible. If still undecided you are probably best advised to start on the alto—you can always transfer to another type of saxophone at a later date.

Try to seek the advice of a teacher or professional player before buying an instrument. Second-hand instruments can sometimes represent excellent value but they need to be expertly assessed.

Part One:
The Foundation Techniques

ASSEMBLING THE INSTRUMENT

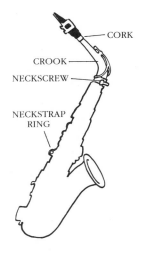

Fig. 1

● Put the neck-strap around your neck and hook it onto the ring which is positioned about halfway down the main body of the saxophone (see Fig. 1).

● First make sure that the neck-screw is untightened and then insert the crook. The crook should point in the same direction as the neck-strap ring. The screw can then be retightened to ensure that the crook does not move.

● Push the mouthpiece onto the cork making sure that the slot or opening is facing towards the floor. If the fit between mouthpiece and cork is too tight you can try applying a little cork grease (see Appendix 4). If it is still too tight you will have to sand down the cork using fine grade sandpaper but proceed with caution—a cork which is too thin can be even more of a problem! If the fit is too loose you can try expanding the cork by holding it close to a flame but be careful that you do not burn it. If this does not remedy the problem you will have to get the crook recorked, in which case make sure you take the mouthpiece with you to check the fit.

● (i) The positioning of the reed on the mouthpiece is particularly important. Reeds must always be handled with great care since they are very delicate and easily damaged.

(ii) First thoroughly moisten the reed by placing the blade or scraped out part in your mouth. This can be done while you are putting the rest of the instrument together.

(iii) The flat part of the reed should now be placed on the flat part of the mouthpiece and positioned so that it is straight in relation to the mouthpiece rails (see Fig. 2).* The tip of the reed should be level with the tip of the mouthpiece when viewed from sideways on (see Fig. 3). One millimetre too high or too low can make blowing much more difficult, so please take care.

Fig. 2

Fig. 3

Fig. 4

*If you find this difficult with the saxophone fully assembled you may remove the crook while you perform this task.

(iv) The ligature should be slightly behind the blade of the reed and should be centralized (see Fig. 4). The screws should be done up until they are finger-tight, but no tighter. If the ligature is the correct size the screw threads will be visible in between the lugs.

Tuning Position

Tuning is affected by the position of the mouthpiece on the cork. The note B on B♭ saxophones or F♯ on E♭ saxophones should correspond to A on a piano, tuning fork or pitch pipe. (An additional tuning note, concert D, is provided on the CD accompaniment for E♭ saxophonists so that—in the early stages—they can tune by fingering B.) If your note is too 'sharp' or high you will need to pull the mouthpiece further off the cork. If it is too 'flat' or low you will need to push on. If you find that you are easily confused as to how pitch is affected by the tuning position remember that short tubes—e.g., trumpet or soprano saxophone—produce high notes, while long tubes—e.g., tuba or baritone saxophone—produce low notes. At first you may find it difficult to establish the correct position. Your teacher or any experienced musician will be able to help. Once established it may be helpful to mark the position with a pen but remember that temperature changes can drastically affect tuning. If the instrument is cold it will be lower in pitch and the mouthpiece will have to be pushed further on, while in hot weather the reverse will be true.

Disassembly

It is important to put the instrument back in its case after you have finished playing. If you leave it assembled for long periods the cork will wear, the crook may not fit so well, the instrument will get dirty and also be exposed to the risk of accidental damage. After you have finished playing you should clean out the inside of the instrument with a pull-through* or cleaning mop (see Appendix 4). Remove the reed; **gently** wipe off excess moisture, and clean out the inside of the mouthpiece with a tissue, taking great care not to rub too hard in the area of the baffle and mouthpiece tip. The reed should be stored in a reed guard (see Appendix 4) or replaced on the mouthpiece, but on no account left loose in the case. Remember to use the mouthpiece cap to protect the reed and mouthpiece tip.

POSTURE

Good posture is vitally important in the playing of musical instruments. The saxophone poses particular problems since a great deal of strain is placed on the neck and it is impossible to adopt a symmetrical body position. Many players who do not initially pay sufficient attention to their posture suffer later on from lower back pain, sciatica or spinal deformities, so be warned!

The quality of the neck-strap can greatly affect how comfortable you feel with the instrument (see Appendix 4). Adjust the neck-strap so that the saxophone comes naturally into your mouth without you having to bring your head down and forward or up and back (see Fig. 5).

Stand with the weight evenly distributed over the feet. Try to avoid thrusting the hips forward, or allowing the neck to be pulled down. The saxophone can be positioned directly in front of the body (Fig. 6) or on the right hand side (Fig. 7).

*This is not possible with the soprano or baritone saxophone.

Fig. 5   Fig. 6   Fig. 7

When sitting down to play make sure to keep your back straight (Fig. 8). Do not slouch or slump. The alto saxophone can be positioned in front (Fig. 9), but it will probably be more comfortable to hold the tenor to the side (Fig. 10).

Fig. 8   Fig. 9   Fig. 10

It is important to understand that the saxophone is **not** held by the hands but rather balanced by the two thumbs, the left thumb pushing forward and to the right, and the right thumb pushing forward and down slightly. This leaves the fingers free to play. To achieve this feeling try swinging the saxophone from side to side, keeping it away from the body (Figs. 11 and 12). Then try swinging it backwards and forwards (Figs. 13 and 14).

Fig. 11   Fig. 12

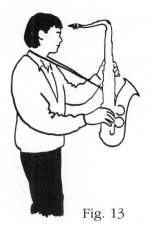

Feel free to move around while you are playing but try to return always to your position of equilibrium. The great tenor saxophone player Sonny Rollins is an excellent model for posture (see photograph on p. 11).

Fig. 13

Fig. 14

FIRST ATTEMPTS

Forget all preconceptions. Put your lips around the mouthpiece and blow in a sustained fashion, as if you were trying to blow out the candles on a birthday cake. Don't hold back! Let go of the breath! If you don't succeed in getting a sound try relaxing the lips or putting a little more mouthpiece in the mouth. This exercise should have demonstrated to you that **the breath produces the sound**. Soon you will be looking at the embouchure in greater depth but do not forget this simple lesson. Your saxophone needs breath like a car needs petrol.

BREATHING EXERCISES

Stand in front of a mirror, preferably one in which you can see yourself from the waist up. Breathe in through the mouth. Most of you will have raised the shoulders and lifted the chest to accomplish this. For the purposes of woodwind playing this is both unnecessary and incorrect. Nor is it how you breathe when you allow unconscious processes to take over.

Exercise 1

Take hold of an average sized hardback book; lie on the floor on your back; place the book on your abdomen and relax. Do not try to breathe in any special way. Simply observe the natural breathing process. Most of you will notice that the book rises as you breathe in and falls as you breathe out. In other words **expansion on inhaling, contraction on exhaling**.

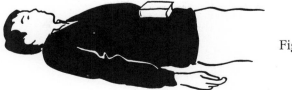

Fig. 15

Now all you have to do is achieve this in a vertical rather than a horizontal position and as a slightly more controlled, conscious process.

Fig. 16

Fig. 17

Exercise 2
- Place the hands on the abdomen (Fig. 16).
- Breathe in through the mouth—a small sip of air rather than a massive gulp. The hands should be pushed out slightly. Exhale.
- Now place the hands on the back (Fig. 17). Breathe in again. You should notice that the hands are pushed backwards. It is as if you were breathing in through two holes in the back underneath the hands. The point is that you are not simply pushing the stomach out but achieving all-round expansion in the area of the waist and lower ribs.

This kind of breathing is called diaphragm breathing. The diaphragm is the powerful muscular floor to the chest cavity. In correct deep breathing the diaphragm moves down to make room as the lungs inflate, thus bringing about the expansion described.

You must now turn your attention to the exhalation. The diaphragm is like a piece of elastic. Left to its own devices it will simply spring back into position and the exhalation will be very short-lived. You might liken this effect to blowing up a balloon and then letting go of it. The balloon flies around the room and within seconds has emptied itself of air. If you let go of your breath in an uncontrolled way your note on the saxophone will be as erratic and short-lived as the flight of the balloon! You must exert a braking influence on the upward movement of the diaphragm, and you do this by contracting the abdominal muscles.

Here is an exercise for practising abdominal control:

Exercise 3
- Breathe in (as described in Exercise 2 above).
- Now breathe out making a loud whispered 'ah' sound. Keep the throat open and relaxed. The 'ah' should be as long and steady as possible—ten or fifteen seconds would be reasonable for a beginner.

What you should notice is that the stomach muscles squeeze more and more firmly until the breath runs out. This effect can be likened to squeezing out a sponge. If you wish to achieve a steady flow of water you must first squeeze gently and then ever more tightly.

TONE QUALITY

It is important for you to understand that the quality of sound you produce on the saxophone will be greatly influenced by the quality of sound you hear in your head. In order to develop your concept of tone-quality you should listen to the great exponents of your instrument as often as possible. One of the great fascinations of the saxophone is its potential for producing many different kinds of tone. Here is a list of some of the most influential exponents of the various saxophones:

Gerry Mulligan

Sonny Rollins

Sidney Bechet

Soprano	*Alto*	*Tenor*	*Baritone*
Sidney Bechet	Johnny Hodges	Coleman Hawkins	Harry Carney
Steve Lacey	Benny Carter	Lester Young	Gerry Mulligan
John Coltrane	Charlie Parker	Ben Webster	Serge Chaloff
Wayne Shorter	Lee Konitz	Don Byas	Lars Gullin
Branford Marsalis	Paul Desmond	Wardell Gray	John Surman
	Art Pepper	Dexter Gordon	
	Cannonball Adderley	Warne Marsh	
	Phil Woods	Stan Getz	
	Ornette Coleman	Zoot Sims	
	David Sanborn	Jimmy Giuffre	
		Sonny Rollins	
		John Coltrane	
		Wayne Shorter	
		Michael Brecker	

Benny Carter &
Coleman Hawkins

For some suggested recordings please consult the discography (Appendix 2).

You should also listen to players of other instruments. Do not confine yourself to jazz! Most great saxophone players have been influenced by other kinds of music. Charlie Parker and John Coltrane are examples of players who listened to a great deal of classical music. Remember Duke Ellington's words: 'There are only two kinds of music—good and bad'. You might improve your tone just as much by listening to a great opera singer like Luciano Pavarotti or a great string player like Pablo Casals or Jascha Heifetz.

THE EMBOUCHURE

Exercise 1

- Whistle. It does not matter if you cannot actually produce much sound—just make the shape. Notice how the inward movement of the muscles at the mouth corners produces a firm but relaxed lip pressure.
- Push down onto your lower lip with one of your fingers while holding this shape and you will notice that it is well supported without the aid of the teeth or jaw. The inward movement of the mouth corners activates the muscles of the lower lip, so crucial in saxophone playing. Notice also that the jaw is in a natural position, neither biting nor unduly dropped, and not thrust forward. You should also feel that the lower lip is stretching slightly up and away from the chin.

Now you are ready to play.

Exercise 2

- Place the top front teeth on the top of the mouthpiece, ensuring they are centralized. The exact distance from the tip of the mouthpiece will vary according to your 'bite' and the dimensions of the mouthpiece, and can only be established by trial and error, but somewhere between ten and fifteen millimetres from the tip would be a reasonable guide. The lower lip should be very slightly turned in, about as much as if you were shaping to say the consonants 'f' or 'v'. Finally, remember to bring the corners of the mouth in towards the centre. Eugene Rousseau has described the embouchure as 'a combination of pronouncing the syllables "V" and "OO",' while Sonny Rollins describes it as the shape your mouth makes when you say 'FOUR'. Do not squeeze too hard. The saxophone embouchure is **firm but relaxed**.
- Now finger the note middle B (see diagram below)* and try to blow as long and steady a tone as possible. At this point many people forget what they have learnt about breathing (see First Attempts, p. 9). You must remember that the embouchure is only a funnel for the breath. It is vital to support the air column by contracting the stomach muscles (see Exercise 3 under Breathing Exercises, pp. 9 & 10).

At this juncture there is no substitute for much long-note practice in front of a mirror, which will provide a visual correlation for your discoveries. Do not neglect this practice or feel that it must be got out of the way so you can get on to 'real music'. If you cannot sustain a steady tone on one note you will never be able to play a tune effectively.

Your first week's practice should consist of ten to fifteen minutes a day—no more, no less—trying to get this B sounding as convincing as possible. You should begin with a few minutes of breathing exercises. For variety you may play middle C, low A, and low G as well. This will be good preparation for your first tunes.

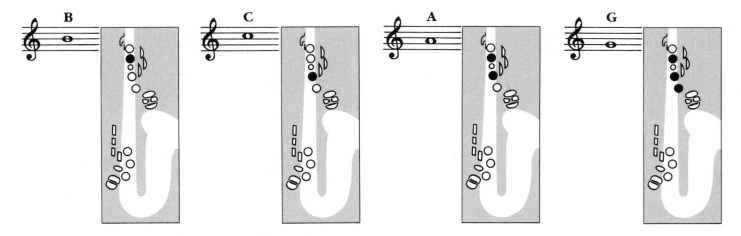

Common Embouchure Faults

- Corners of the mouth pointing down, leading to a weak and unsteady sound.
- Corners of the mouth pulling back. This is a common fault with those players who have already played the clarinet and tends to produce a restricted sound.
- Chin collapsing upwards towards the lip. This usually results in a feeble tone.
- Not enough mouthpiece in the mouth, producing a wavering and muffled sound.
- Too much mouthpiece in the mouth, producing a raucous tone.
- Not enough lip turned in, producing a loss of control.
- Too much lip turned in, also leading to a weak and unsteady sound.
- Thrusting the jaw forward, which can produce a raucous tone or general lack of control.

*Keys shaded in black should be held down to play the required note.

Another vital foundation technique for playing the saxophone is tonguing. The tongue is the saxophonist's equivalent of a violin bow, or a drumstick. It allows you to start notes clearly and precisely, to repeat notes and to produce subtle variations of phrasing.

Exercise 1

Imagine that you are a ventriloquist.* Sing any note that is comfortably within your vocal range using the syllable 'doo'. Repeat the 'doo' sound slowly and in a steady rhythm using **one breath only**. You should produce a continuous sound as if you were singing one long note. Look at yourself in the mirror while doing this. There should be **no movement of lips, teeth or jaw**. Only the front part of the tongue moves. You will find that the tongue movements have to be very delicate to achieve this. It is also important that the tongue moves **straight up and down**.

Now you will try to apply this movement to the saxophone, using a stage-by-stage process. The following exercises should be practised in sequence.

*I am grateful to my first teacher, Don Rendell, for this exercise.

Exercise 2a

- Blow the note middle B and hold it steady for a few seconds.
- Move the tongue up to touch only the edge of the reed (Fig. 18a) and hold it there for a few seconds, still maintaining breath pressure. Usually it will be just behind the tip of the tongue that makes contact with the reed, but if you have a larger or smaller tongue it may be more comfortable to touch the reed with a different part (Figs. 18b and c). Aim for what feels most natural. You should experience a kind of bottled-up sensation.
- Pull the mouthpiece out of the mouth. There should be a rush of air, rather like air being released from a tyre. If not, you are failing to maintain the pressure of air behind the tongue which is vital for good tonguing.

Fig. 18

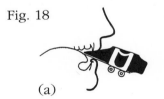      

(a)   (b)   (c)

Exercise 2b

- Blow the note middle B and hold it steady for a few seconds.
- Move the tongue up to the reed and hold it there for a few seconds.
- Move the tongue back down to its original position, slightly below the reed. The note should sound again immediately. If it does not you have probably forgotten about maintaining the breath pressure!

> **Exercise 2c**
> - Blow the note middle B and hold it steady for a few seconds.
> - Move the tongue up to the reed and then immediately down again. The tongue should move lightly and effortlessly, in much the same way as it did for Exercise 1. Listen to your sound. The action of the tongue should not disturb the tone-quality in any way nor constrict the throat, which should be kept open and relaxed.

> **Exercise 3**
> You should now practise blowing a single note and tonguing at regular intervals, starting at speeds of about one note every four seconds. Slow practice is the key to mastering most things in music. It gives you plenty of time to become aware of what you are doing.

The Attack

For **starting** notes with the tongue the procedure is as follows:
1. Breathe in.
2. Set the embouchure and keep it **absolutely still**.
3. Move the tongue up to the reed in the manner already described.
4. Bring the air to just behind the tongue. You should experience the same bottled-up sensation described in Exercise 2a above. The stomach muscles should be firm, supporting the air column.
5. Move the tongue down. The note should sound immediately. You may find it helpful to imagine you are saying 'doo'.

Stopping the Note

The note is stopped by moving the tongue up to touch the edge of the reed. You will have to do this very gently to achieve a clean end to the note.

Some Common Faults

- Touching the underneath of the reed.
- Moving the tongue backwards and forwards rather than up and down.
- Moving the tongue too much.
- Moving the embouchure when you tongue, resulting in distortion of the tone.
- Not maintaining breath pressure.

Summary

- You should touch only the edge of the reed.
- The tongue should move up and down (no more than about five millimetres in either direction).
- Touch the reed as gently as possible. If you can touch it any more gently you are touching too hard.
- Move the tongue as little as possible and keep the tongue close to the edge of the reed.
- Maintain breath pressure.

During the second week you should first practise long notes and then the tonguing exercises.

- The fleshy pad at the end of the finger should make contact with the key (see Fig. 19).
- The fingers should be gently curved (see Figs. 20 and 21), not flat or contracted.

Fig. 19

Fig. 20 *A 'birds-eye' view of the right hand on the saxophone – showing the gentle curvature of the fingers*

Fig. 21 *Left-hand position*

- The fingers move by means of a hammer action which is initiated at the knuckle joint.
- The fingers should stay as close as possible to the keys. Do not waste energy!
- In order for the fingers to stay relaxed and move efficiently it is necessary that the neck muscles, shoulder joints, elbows and wrists should also be relaxed.

You have now been taught the vital foundation techniques of the saxophone. Whatever kind of music you play these techniques for producing and articulating the sound will always be involved, so practise them diligently.

FURTHER STUDY

Reading:

LARRY TEAL, *The Art of Saxophone Playing*. The chapters on breathing technique, embouchure, tone-quality, intonation and attack and release are particularly relevant.

Part Two:
Playing the Music

CHAPTER 1

The Staff

Music is written on a staff (plural, staves) or group of five parallel lines.

Pitch, or how high or low a note is (see under Tuning Position, p. 7) is indicated by the position of that note on the staff—the higher the note the higher it is on the staff. Music uses a seven letter alphabet up to G to describe the pitch of notes:

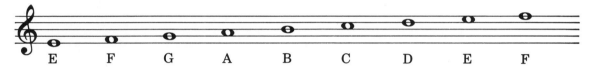

E F G A B C D E F

Mnemonics can be useful in helping to recall these note positions. For example, the initial letters of **E**very **G**ood **B**oy **D**eserves **F**avour for the lines and the word **FACE** for the spaces.

Clefs

The sign at the beginning of the staff is a treble clef sign. The word clef is derived from the French word for a key. It shows the position of a particular note on the staff and thus is the key for finding the position of all the other notes. All saxophone music is written in the treble clef, 𝄞 a stylized form of the letter G, curling to indicate the position of that note. Certain other instruments use different clefs. For example, the double bass uses the bass clef 𝄢 ; while the viola uses the C clef 𝄡 and the piano generally uses treble clef for the right hand and bass clef for the left hand.

Bars and Bar-Lines

Vertical lines written across the staff are bar-lines. The spaces between the bar-lines are called bars. Bars divide the music into easily recognizable units of time. They do not represent stops or pauses. They simply make counting easier, and counting, as you will see, is vital in the reading of music.

Time Signatures

If you look at the beginning of 'Blues for Beginners' (p. 18) you will see two numbers written one over the other. This is the time signature. It can be thought of as a fraction, the top figure or numerator telling us the number of beats in the bar and the bottom figure or denominator the kind of beat. In this case there are four **quarter** or **crotchet** beats in each bar.

Note Durations

Crotchets, ♩ minims ♩ and semibreves ○ are the note durations that you will encounter in your first pieces and exercises. A minim is twice the length of a crotchet and a semi-breve is twice the length of a minim. In the USA the terms are respectively quarter note, half note and whole note which express the mathematical relationship between the note values more clearly.

Pulse and Rhythm

Look at 'Blues for Beginners'. Count in groups of four beats and clap on every first beat, holding the hands together to express the duration of the semibreve,* which is four beats.

Clap: x   x   x   x

Count: 1 2 3 4 1 2 3 4 1 2 3 4 1 2 3 4, etc.

What you are doing is counting the **pulse** and clapping the **rhythm**.

Rhythm is the organization of notes in time and is not **necessarily** regular, although in this instance it is. Pulse—often referred to as 'the beat'—is usually felt rather than heard and is nearly always regular. It is very often what we dance to in music. Pulse determines the speed of the music and helps us to measure the distance between notes. Now you should practise counting and clapping with the CD. The claps should coincide precisely with the notes of the saxophone. This procedure of counting and clapping before playing should be carefully adhered to throughout the book. Rhythm is the most basic element of music, and it is vital to master this aspect of each piece before proceeding further.

Taking a Breath

The commas written above the stave are suggested breathing places. Breaths should not be taken where doing so would destroy the flow of the music. There is a parallel here with speech, where breaths are generally taken at the end of sentences or phrases, except by small children who are still learning the art!

In 'Blues for Beginners' there are no spaces between the notes. In such cases you must create a breathing space by cutting the note before the breath mark slightly short. You should take small sips of air at regular intervals. Most beginners drastically overestimate the amount of breath they need—small amounts will be sufficient provided that the breath is adequately supported by the stomach muscles. Leave the top teeth where they are and inhale either through the mouth corners or by dropping the lower jaw. **Do not breathe through your nose**!

The following exercise may help you to become accustomed to the correct mode of breathing. Breathe at the commas. The rhythm should be regular and undisturbed by the taking of the breath. Count slowly and steadily.

Count aloud: 1 2 3 4 1 2 3 4 ' 1 2 3 4 1 2 3 4 ', etc.

Metronome Markings

Now you are ready to play 'Blues for Beginners'. The instruction ♩ = 88 at the beginning of the piece is a metronome marking, meaning that the music is to be played at a speed of around 88 beats per minute. A metronome is a device which marks the pulse by means of a regular click and would be a worthwhile purchase (see Appendix 4).

---

*Claps can only indicate the position of notes in time - not their duration.

Fingering positions for the pieces in this chapter and the following one are shown in the diagrams on p. 12.

see diagrams on p. 12.

Blues for Beginners**

Rests

The next two pieces introduce minims, and minim and semibreve rests. A minim is worth two beats in 4/4 time. The minim rest sits on the third line, measuring from the bottom of the staff upwards and represents two beats of silence, while the semibreve rest hangs from the fourth line, representing four beats of silence. Silence in music is just as important as sound, so make sure you count the rests carefully.

There is an optional harmony part to 'A la Mode', which can be played by a teacher or more advanced player.

A la Mode

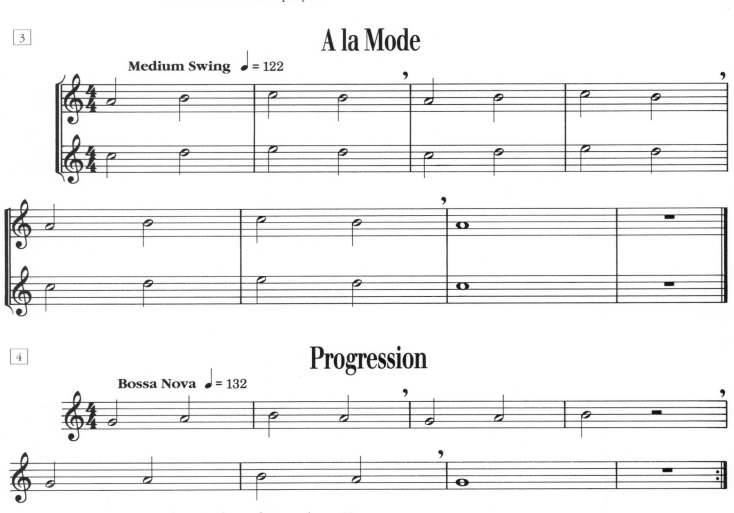

Progression

*These numbers refer to tracks on CD.

**All pieces are original compositions by John O'Neill unless otherwise indicated.

CHAPTER 2

Riffs

'Out for the Count' is a twelve-bar blues consisting of a single phrase which is repeated three times. Short repeated phrases of this type are known as riffs. They were often used by big bands during the swing era as a means of building excitement, with different riffs sometimes being assigned to each section of the band. The Count Basie band of the 1930s is a perfect example.

Crotchets

This is the first piece to use crotchets, which are worth one beat each in 4/4 time.

The 'Pick-Up'

You will notice that there are just two crotchets before the first bar-line, in spite of the fact that the time signature indicates four beats to each bar. These two crotchets are an example of an anacrusis, usually referred to by jazz musicians as a 'pick-up'. An anacrusis is an unstressed note or group of notes at the beginning of a musical phrase. In this instance, the first strong accent falls on the C and not the G or A.

Repeats

At the end of the piece is a double bar preceded by two dots. This means that you repeat from the beginning. There is only one repeat unless otherwise indicated. In this case, because of the anacrusis, there are only two beats' rest in the bar before the repeat:

Out for the Count

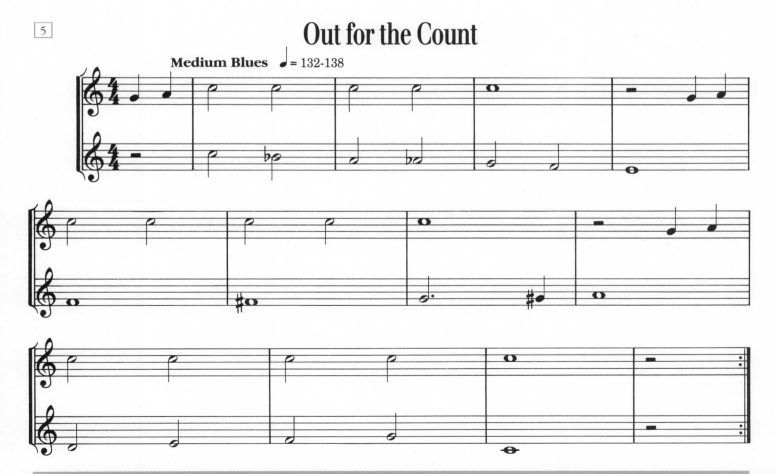

Slurs

The curved lines above the notes in 'Times Remembered' are **slurs**. You should tongue only the first note within a slur group. For example, in the opening two bars you tongue only the first note.

6

Times Remembered

7

P.M.

8

Third Attempt

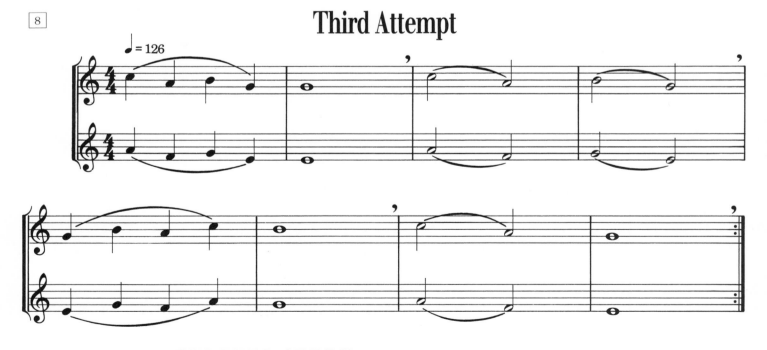

FURTHER STUDY

Listening:

COUNT BASIE, 'Jumping at the Woodside' from *Swinging the Blues*. A classic example of the use of riffs.

CHAPTER 3

The four tunes in this section contain two new notes—low F and E. In order to produce these notes a slight increase in support from the stomach muscles will be necessary. The embouchure should be kept completely still, particularly while tonguing. Failure to observe these points will often result in an unstable tone, with the note perhaps jumping into the next register.

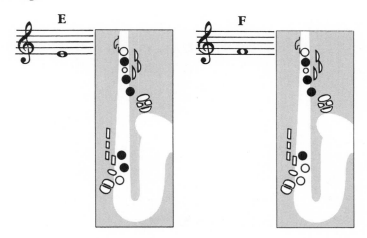

Dynamic Markings

The new pieces also contain dynamic markings. They are used to indicate volume levels within a piece and are abbreviations of Italian words:

Marking	Italian word	Meaning
p	*piano*	quiet
mf	*mezzoforte*	medium loud
f	*forte*	loud

Crotchet Rests

The sign ⁊ in 'Flat 5' is a crotchet or quarter-note rest. It represents one beat of silence in 4/4 time.

Ties

In 'Flat 5' you will notice that the last two notes are connected by a curved line. This is called a **tie**. It has the effect of joining the two notes together as one, so you do not tongue the second G, but simply extend it by four extra beats. Do not confuse ties with slurs. A tie always connects notes of the same pitch, whereas a slur connects notes of different pitch.

9

Flat 5

Interstellar

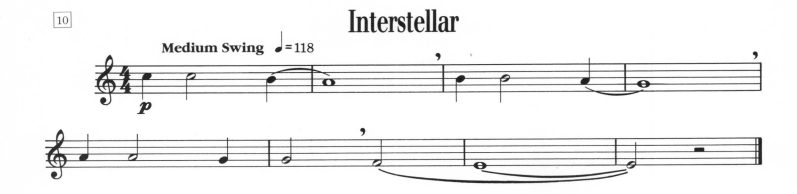

Syncopation

'251' is made more difficult by the presence of **syncopation**, which can be defined as the placing of accents where you would not normally expect to find them—the effect being one of rhythmic surprise. Much of the vitality of jazz derives from the extensive use of syncopated rhythms. In this example it is the fourth beats of the first, third and fifth bars which are syncopated.

251

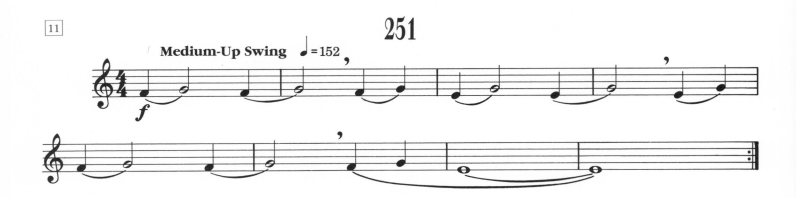

In 'Home Bass' you will notice after the first two crotchets a double bar with two dots placed **after** it. This is an indication of where you repeat **from**.

Home Bass

FURTHER STUDY

It is important that you spend some of your practice time playing by ear. Try to memorize some of the tunes you have learnt so far and play them without the music. Inventing your own tunes would also be a good idea.

Play the lower part of 'Third Attempt' from the previous chapter (p. 20).

Sharps, Semitones and Accidentals

In 'James' you will find middle C sharp for the first time. This note is indicated by a **sharp** sign ♯ written in front of the C. A sharp means the note is raised by one **semitone**, which is the distance between one note and its nearest neighbour note, i.e., the smallest interval 'officially' recognized in the mainstream of Western music. Signs which alter notes in this way are called **accidentals**. Accidentals affect every note of the same pitch in the bar, so in bar 3 of 'James' **both** C's are sharp.

This tune is an example of the bossa-nova rhythm, made famous in jazz by the early sixties recordings of tenor saxophonist Stan Getz.

Dotted Notes

The first note is a minim with a dot placed after it. A dot placed after a note extends its duration by half as much again. A dotted minim is therefore worth three beats (2 + 1).

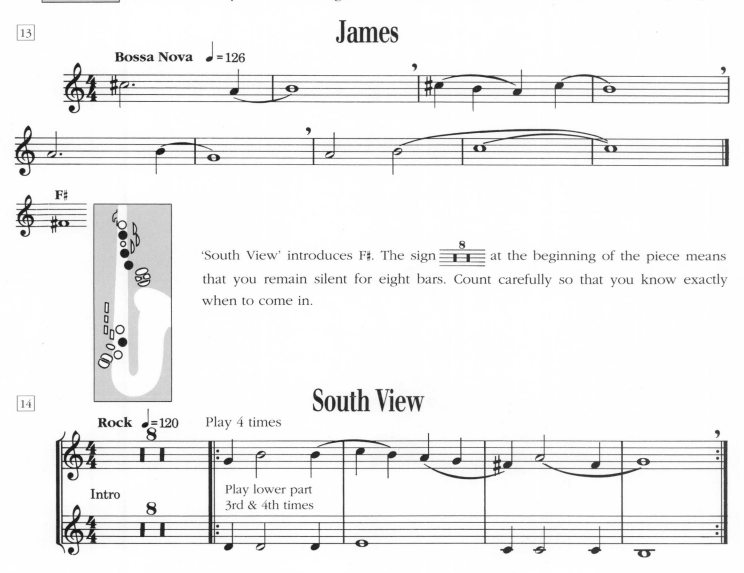

James

'South View' introduces F♯. The sign ▬ at the beginning of the piece means that you remain silent for eight bars. Count carefully so that you know exactly when to come in.

South View

The Natural Sign

In 'Minor Problem' the second note of bars 1, 3 and 5 is preceded by another kind of accidental, the **natural** sign ♮, which cancels any previous accidentals in the bar.

Minor Problem

Medium Groove ♩=126

Accents

'Devil Music' introduces accents. The sign ∧ over the first note is a short accent, meaning that the note is to be attacked hard and then stopped short of its full written value.* The sign > below the F♯ in bar 1 means that the beginning of the note should be played with extra emphasis. This is achieved by a slight 'kick' of the stomach muscles, similar to what happens when you cough. The line written above and below the notes in bars 9 and 10 means that these notes should be held for their full value.

The Pause

The sign written over the last note is a pause, sometimes called a *fermata*, which has the effect of prolonging the note beyond its written value, at the discretion of the performer or musical director.

Devil Music

Slow Medium Blues ♩=120

Stan Getz

FURTHER STUDY

Listening:

STAN GETZ, *Jazz Samba; Stan Getz and Joao Gilberto*. Both of these records are classic examples of the use of the bossa-nova rhythm in jazz.

*Note for teachers: this is **not** the same as the classical staccato, which is lighter and shorter.

The Break

One of the major technical problems of saxophone playing is crossing the 'break', or moving to middle register D from the notes below. This involves considerable finger coordination and the exercise below will be a useful preparatory study.

Play the exercise slowly and evenly, with good tone, concentrating on the following points:

● The ball of the thumb stays in contact with the left-hand thumb button at all times. You must operate the octave key by bending the top joint of the thumb (see Figs. 22 and 23) and **not** by lifting or sliding the thumb.

Fig. 22 *Thumb position: octave key shut*

Fig. 23 *Thumb position: octave key open*

● It is essential to keep the embouchure still. Resist any temptation to tighten the embouchure as you pass from C to D.
● The throat must stay open and relaxed.
● Support for the air column from the abdominal muscles must be maintained.
● Do not be put off if the D sounds slightly muffled. Because of the number of pads that are being held down, it does have a denser tone quality than the C. As you become more experienced you will learn to compensate for this.
● The notes should be slurred throughout, with the exception of the initial attack note.
● For the purposes of the exercise you can keep the three right-hand fingers down while playing C. This will not drastically affect the pitch of the note and enables you to concentrate on the left hand, where the principal difficulty lies.

Once you are able to play the exercise smoothly you will be ready to try moving the right-hand fingers as well.

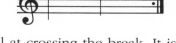

Do not be discouraged if you are not immediately successful at crossing the break. It is a technical challenge even for more advanced players.

'Breaking Point' will provide similar technical practice with CD accompaniment.

Breaking Point

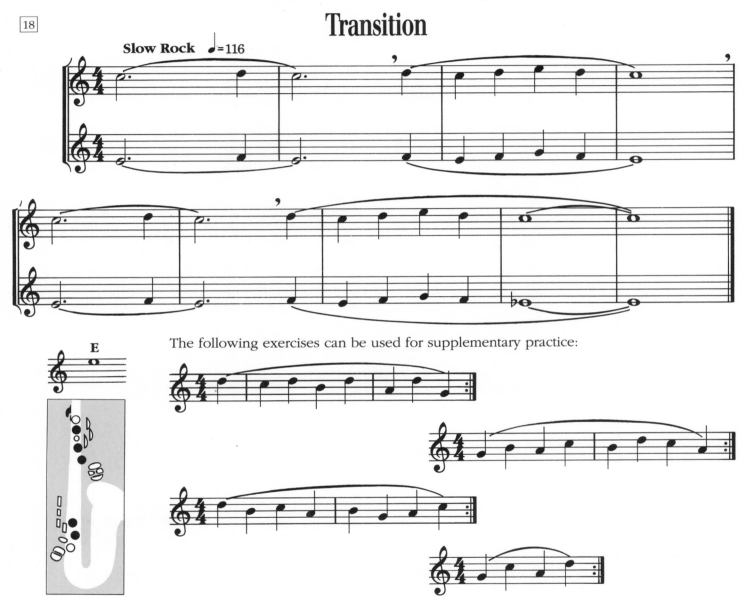

'Transition' introduces E above the break (see diagram below).

The following exercises can be used for supplementary practice:

Sylvie's Dance

K.O.

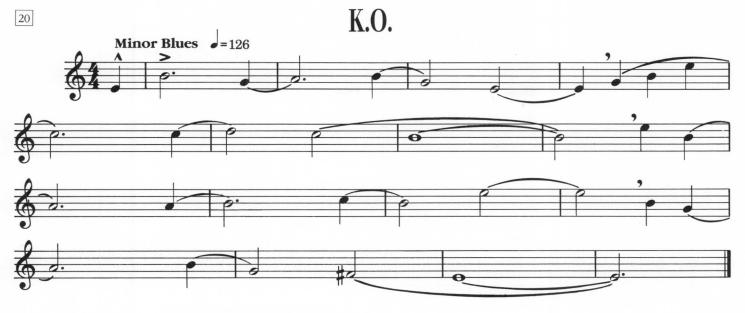

Minor Blues ♩=126

FURTHER STUDY

Playing:

Play the lower part of 'A la Mode' from Chapter 1 (p. 18).

CHAPTER 6

You are advised to reread the remarks at the beginning of Chapter 3 concerning low notes (p. 21). If difficulties persist experiment with softer reeds or putting a little more mouthpiece in the mouth. If neither approach has any effect it is possible that your instrument is leaking. Have it thoroughly checked by your teacher, a professional player or a competent repairer.

Ledger lines

Low C is placed on a ledger line. Ledger lines are extra lines placed above or below the stave to allow for the notation of notes in the highest and lowest registers.

Fig. 24 *Technique for low C*

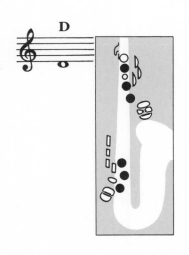

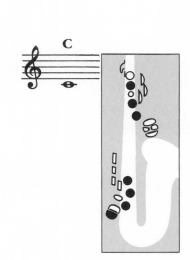

Low Note Exercise

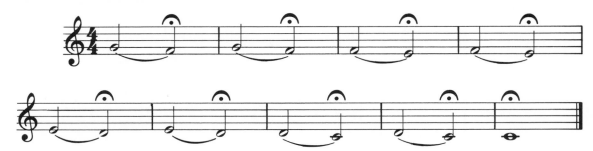

First and Second Time Bars

'The Bottom Line' introduces first and second time bars. These are frequently used to save space on repeats. The second time bars are played as an **alternative**—never in addition—to the first time bars on the repeat.

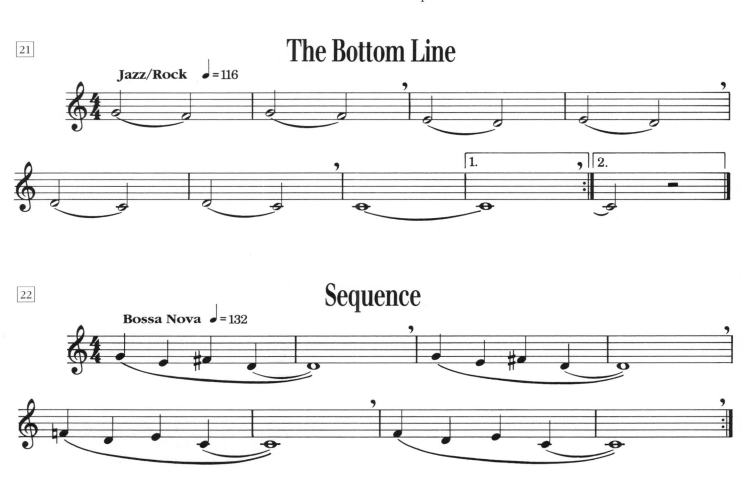

21

The Bottom Line

Jazz/Rock ♩=116

22

Sequence

Bossa Nova ♩=132

23

Fourths

♩=124

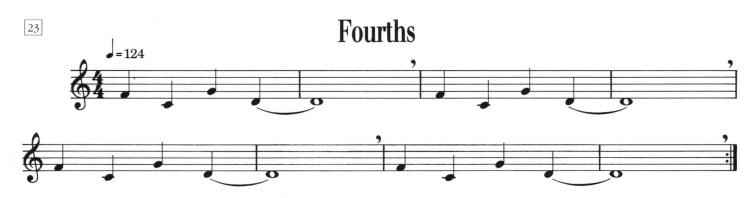

Scales

The word scale is derived from the Italian 'scala' meaning 'staircase' or 'ladder'. It is a series of single notes moving up or down in steps.

Chords

A **chord** is a combination of notes sounding together. Simple three-note chords are known as triads.

It is impossible to play chords on the saxophone in the way that a keyboard player or guitarist can, although some players have experimented with **multiphonics**—the playing of more than one note by using alternative fingerings and advanced blowing techniques.

Arpeggios

An arpeggio is a chord played **melodically**, sounding the notes one after the other, rather than **harmonically**, playing the notes simultaneously.

Scales and arpeggios are the 'nuts and bolts' of most jazz improvisation although, to achieve good results, creative rather than mechanical use must be made of them! Below are the C major scale and arpeggio.* They should be committed to memory and played slowly—maximum speed sixty beats per minute. Strive for rhythmic and tonal evenness. Scales and arpeggios should initially be played slurred to develop smooth technique. Once this has been mastered they may be tongued as well.

Flats

In the fingering exercises the flat sign ♭ is introduced. When placed before a note as an accidental it means that the note is to be played a semitone **lower**.

Side B♭ vs. Bis B♭

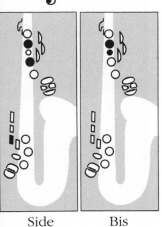

Side   Bis

B♭ is probably the most debated fingering on the saxophone, there being several different ways of playing it. The two main options, namely side B♭ and 'bis' B♭, are introduced in this chapter. ('Bis' is French for 'twice', implying an alternative.) Discussions with professional players will reveal a considerable division of opinion as to which is the best fingering for a given musical situation. You are therefore advised to practise both fingerings until you have developed your own preferences. Keep an open mind— as you learn new notes you may find your opinions change.

You will see that to play 'bis' you are required to depress two keys simultaneously using the first finger only (see Fig. 27). One important point to remember is that the first finger can remain in this position while playing any notes that involve depressing the

*The construction of major and minor scales and arpeggios is discussed at greater length in Chapter 21 (p. 67).

first two fingers of the left hand. In the second exercise below, for example, you can keep the first finger in position for bis B♭ while playing the G.

In the fourth exercise you will have to roll the first finger from bis B♭ to B natural (see Figs. 26 and 27) if you decide to use this instead of the side fingering.

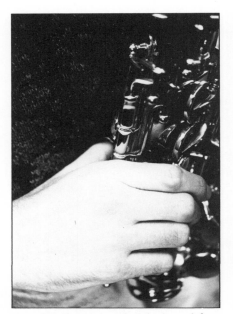

Fig. 25 *Position of right hand for Side B♭*

Fig. 26 *Rolling from B . . .*

Fig. 27 *. . . to bis B♭*

N.B. The last two exercises can be played as a duet, with the further option of one part being played an octave higher.

Key Signatures

When accidentals are placed immediately after the clef sign as in 'Roberto' they form a **key signature**, which tells you which notes are to be played sharp or flat for the duration of the entire piece rather than for just a single bar. In this case the placement of the

24

Roberto

Bossa Nova ♩=126

flat sign on the middle line of the stave means that all B's are to be played flat unless otherwise indicated by an accidental.

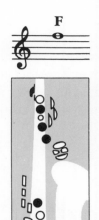

Enharmonic Notes

'Romancing' introduces F above the break, and D♭, which is another name for the note C♯. The note in between C and D is both one semitone higher than C (C♯) and one semitone lower than D (D♭). Notes like C♯ and D♭ which can be named in two ways are said to be **enharmonic notes**.*

D.S. al Coda

The term *D.S. al Coda,* an abbreviation of *Dal Segno al Coda,* means literally 'from the sign to the tail'. A coda is an extra section which is added to a piece. When you meet this instruction you repeat from the sign 𝄋 and then go to the coda at the coda sign ⊕.

From this tune onwards detailed articulation** and dynamic markings have been omitted. Jazz is a highly personal music and you should work towards developing your own conceptions of tone and phrasing. To this end you should experiment with many different possibilities for phrasing and expression. There is more than one 'right way'. Listening carefully to recordings of great saxophone players will also be highly instructive.

*For reasons of musical 'grammar' it is essential that the student learns to think of enharmonic notes in **both** ways.
**Articulation markings are those which indicate where, and where not, to tongue.

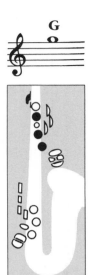

CHAPTER 9

The fingering exercises and 'Blue Jean' introduce G above the break. As you extend the range upwards it is essential that you do not tighten the embouchure or constrict the throat muscles. The notes will speak freely and easily, provided that you support the air column with the abdominal muscles. Try to achieve the feeling of your sound 'floating on air'.

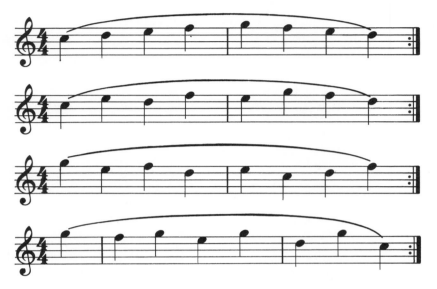

N.B. The second and third exercises can be played as a duet.

Blue Jean

Improvisation

Now you are ready to try improvising for the first time. Here is a five-note scale, also known as a **pentatonic scale**, which will serve as your source material. It would be a good idea to learn it by heart before attempting to improvise with it.

Play the backing track again, but this time play whatever you feel using the scale notes only.* You need not worry about playing any 'wrong' notes, since all of the notes in the scale will sound fine wherever you play them.

Most beginner improvisers make the mistake of neglecting the rhythmic aspect of their playing. The following exercises should help with this problem:

● Clap out a solo, or tap one on your legs or on a table top. Be as adventurous as you like, but try to maintain a strong rhythmic feeling in what you do, like a good jazz drummer.

*The scale notes may be played in any register of the saxophone, so you can also play low G, E, D and C.

- Once you are happy about clapping a solo return to the saxophone and try improvising again but this time think of the scale as a set of 'tuned drums', trying to retain the strong rhythmic feeling you had while you were clapping.

This exercise should have helped you to realize that **the most important element of any jazz solo is rhythm**.

Relative Keys

Below are the scales and arpeggios of F major and D minor. You will notice that they share the same key signature. They are known as relative keys. They contain the same notes, except the seventh note of the D minor scale is sharpened, shown as required by an accidental and not in the key signature. There are various forms of the minor scale, this particular one being known as the harmonic minor. Do not skip scale practice; its importance will become more apparrent as you progress through the book. If you wish to become a good improviser knowledge of major and minor scales and arpeggios is vital. Remember, they should be committed to memory.

F major

D harmonic minor

CHAPTER 10

A♭/G♯ and E♭/D♯ are more examples of enharmonic notes.

Fig. 28 *Technique for E♭/D♯*

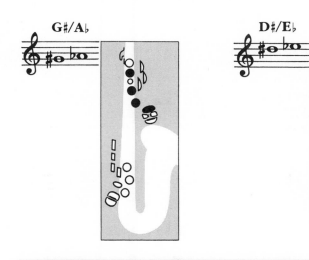

Both notes involve coordination of the two weakest fingers. The fingering exercises are designed to strengthen these. Play them slowly at first (♩ = 60) and then gradually increase the tempo.

The Chromatic Scale

Now that you have learnt Ab/G♯ and Eb/D♯ you are able to practise the **chromatic scale**, in which one moves by semitone steps from any note to the same note in the next register. The example below shows a chromatic scale starting on G. In order to give you more practice with enharmonic notes I have written sharps in the ascending version and flats in the descending version of the scale.

Alternative F♯ and C

While practising the chromatic scale you may wish to experiment with the alternative fingerings for F♯ and C. I use these alternatives mainly as trill fingerings, but some players favour them for chromatic movement as well. As with all alternative fingerings the most intelligent solution is to practise both ways and then decide for yourself according to the musical situation. It is important, however, also to be aware that some of the alternative fingerings affect the pitch and tone quality of the note.

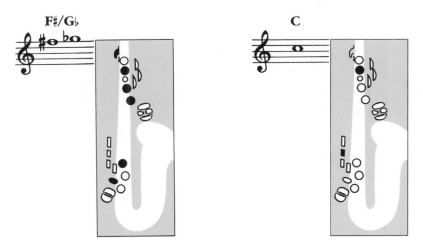

'Bird Waltz' is a chromatic blues inspired by the music of Charlie Parker (1920–1955), sometimes known as Bird. Arguably the greatest of all alto saxophone players, he was one of the creators of Bebop, a jazz style which dominated the 1940s, and has continued to exert a powerful influence on contemporary music.

3/4 Time

This tune introduces 3/4 or waltz time, in which there are three crotchet beats to each bar, with a strong emphasis on the first beat. 3/4 time was rarely heard in jazz before the 1950s. It has become much more popular since then, and is particularly associated with the music of the lyrical and highly influential pianist Bill Evans.

Transposition

I have written 'Bird Waltz' in two keys, C and B major. The process of moving a tune into a different key is known as **transposition.*** Transposition is one of the most effective ways of improving your knowledge of keys, getting to know your instrument and training your ear.

At the end of 'A Song for Sophie' you can improvise using the pentatonic scale indicated. The sign ⁒ indicates a whole-bar repeat.

Use of Space

Make sure you do not clutter your solos with too many notes. The best jazz musicians know how to make effective use of **space**. There are two ways of creating space in a solo—one is by using silence and the other is by playing notes of longer duration. In either case you will find you have more time to be aware of what you and—just as importantly—the other musicians are doing. As a result your playing should become more relaxed, expressive and coherent. Trumpeter Miles Davis is a fine example of someone who uses space quite brilliantly.

*More information about transposition can be found in Appendix 6.

A Song for Sophie

FURTHER STUDY

Playing:

As an exercise in transposition try playing any of the tunes you have played so far starting on a different note. Other good material for transposition would be simple folk tunes or nursery rhymes.

Listening:

CHARLIE PARKER, 'Blues for Alice' from *Charlie Parker* (Compact Jazz series).

BILL EVANS, 'Waltz for Debbie' from *At the Village Vanguard*. A beautiful example of a jazz waltz.

MILES DAVIS, *Kind Of Blue*. Listen in particular to the trumpet solos for examples of the use of space.

Reading:

ROSS RUSSELL, *Bird Lives*.

GARY GIDDINS, *Celebrating Bird: The Triumph of Charlie Parker*.

ROBERT REISNER, *Bird: The Legend of Charlie Parker*.

Viewing:

'Bird' directed by Clint Eastwood.

Miles Davis

Sight-reading is only one of the many skills a good jazz musician must acquire. A discriminating ear is possibly the most vital asset, since effective improvisation depends on being able to translate the ideas in your head onto the instrument as quickly as possible.

Ear Training

A lucky minority seem to develop fantastic aural perception at a very early age. At the other end of the spectrum true 'tone-deafness' is much rarer than people imagine. For the vast majority in between these extremes aural training can produce remarkable results.

Intervals

One important skill is the ability to recognize and sing intervals. Intervals are a means of expressing the distance between one note and another. You should begin to develop your sense of this by learning to sing the intervals of the major and minor scales. The chart below indicates the names of these intervals in the major scale, measuring them from the first note, also known as the **tonic**. The subsequent degrees of the scale are expressed as Roman numerals:

Major Scale (C)

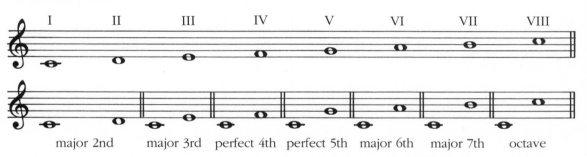

The intervals between successive degrees of the harmonic minor scale and the tonic are the same, except between I-III (which is a minor third) and I-VI (a minor sixth); these two intervals are a semitone smaller than their major counterparts:

Harmonic Minor Scale (C)

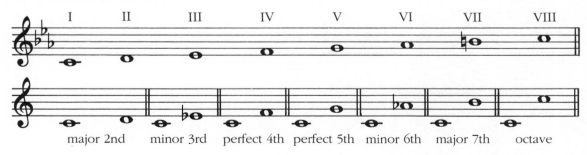

It is important to realize that the intervals are the same for every key. For example, the distance between the tonic and the fifth note of any major or minor scale, measured as an ascending interval, is always a perfect fifth.

In the exercises which follow try not to be too self-conscious about your singing. Accuracy of pitch is more important than tone quality. Singing will help your saxophone playing and vice-versa—the technique of supporting the breath and relaxing the throat is almost identical.

Once you are confident with fifths you can progress to other intervals. A recommended order of study is: perfect fifth, perfect fourth, octave, major second, major third, minor third, major sixth, minor sixth, major seventh.

Some students find it helpful to use mnemonics for the intervals. For example, the first two notes of 'Oh When the Saints Go Marching In' are a major third apart. Some other possibly helpful mnemonics are 'Here Comes the Bride' for a perfect fourth, 'Twinkle Twinkle Little Star' for a perfect fifth, and 'My Bonny Lies Over the Ocean' for a major sixth. You might wish to substitute some tunes of your own—the more familiar the better.

Having developed an ability to sing ascending intervals, you should next practise descending intervals. These are named in the major and harmonic minor scales as follows:

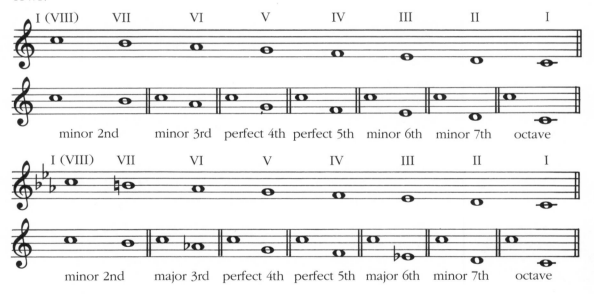

Inversions

The interval which measures the distance between the same pair of named notes but in the opposite direction, e.g., from C **down** to D rather than **up** to D (or from C **up** to G instead of **down** to G) is known as an inversion. From the above examples you can see that the original interval and its inversion always add up to nine, e.g., seconds become sevenths, and fourths become fifths; major intervals become minor when inverted and minor intervals become major; perfect intervals remain perfect.

You should practise singing descending intervals by adapting the exercises given above. A suggested order of study is: perfect fourth, octave, minor third, minor second, perfect fifth, major third, minor sixth, major sixth, minor seventh.

Playing By Ear

Playing by ear is one of the most enjoyable and effective ways of improving your aural perception. Any material will do—nursery rhymes, hymns, folk tunes, songs you hear on the radio, T.V. themes, advertising jingles—but the most relevant exercise would be to get hold of jazz recordings and learn to play jazz tunes. You will also develop your sound, sense of time and phrasing by listening to the jazz masters in this way.

If you cannot afford to buy the records visit your local music library, which will often contain an excellent record collection. This is a good way to become familiar with the jazz heritage. You should start with simple melodies—ballads by Ben Webster or Paul Desmond for example. Recordings by singers, for example the 1950s' recordings of Frank Sinatra, are also good source material.

Proceed as follows:

1. Play the recording several times.
2. Sing the melody with the recording, trying to imitate as closely as possible with your voice the inflections of the saxophone. This technique of imitating instrumental sounds with the voice is known as **scat-singing**. Louis Armstrong, Ella Fitzgerald, Chet Baker, Al Jarreau and Bobby McFerrin are five of the very best scat-singers.
3. Sing the melody without the recording—this is much harder!
4. Play the melody with the recording. This will develop the ability to translate what you hear in your head to your fingers—a vital skill for musicians who wish to improvise.
5. Play the melody without the recording.

You may find this difficult at first but please persevere—it becomes easier with practice. This sort of exercise will probably develop your playing more than anything else.

Later on you can progress to more intricate melodies and even jazz solos. Some sort of device for slowing the music down to half-speed is invaluable. This could be either a reel-to-reel tape-recorder which records at both $7\frac{1}{2}$ and $3\frac{3}{4}$ ips or a record player which slows down to 16 rpm, preferably with sliding pitch control to facilitate tuning.* Both of these items can be relatively cheaply acquired through small-ad pages of newspapers, junk shops or second-hand audio equipment shops. The ability to slow down solos opens up a whole world of difficult music to your ears. Charlie Parker is said to have used this method to study the music of his idol Lester Young.

FURTHER STUDY

Playing:

This game can be played with your teacher or another saxophonist: Position yourselves so that neither player can see the other's fingerings, and take it in turns to sound any note. The other player must try to sound the same note in response. By practising regularly at this game you will be surprised how easy it becomes to find the correct note on first attempt.

Reading:

PAUL HINDEMITH, *Elementary Training for Musicians*. Not for the faint-hearted! This book contains at least two years' study. But worth the effort.

Listening:

LOUIS ARMSTRONG, 'Basin Street Blues' from *Hot 5 and Hot 7*.
ELLA FITZGERALD, 'Rockin' in Rhythm' from *Sings the Duke Ellington Songbook*.
CHET BAKER, 'But Not For Me' from *The Touch of Your Lips*.
AL JARREAU, 'Roof Garden' and 'Blue Rondo a la Turk' from *Breakin' Away*
BOBBY McFERRIN, 'Walkin' from *Spontaneous Inventions*.
The above recordings are all examples of scat-singing.

Louis Armstrong

*Cassette players with a slow-down facility are also available.

CHAPTER 12

Registers of the Saxophone

The saxophone has three registers. The lower register is from bottom B♭ to middle C♯. From middle D to A♭ the action of the thumb on the octave mechanism opens the lower octave key, producing the middle register, while from high A to top F and beyond the same thumb action opens the upper octave key, situated on the crook, producing the upper register.*

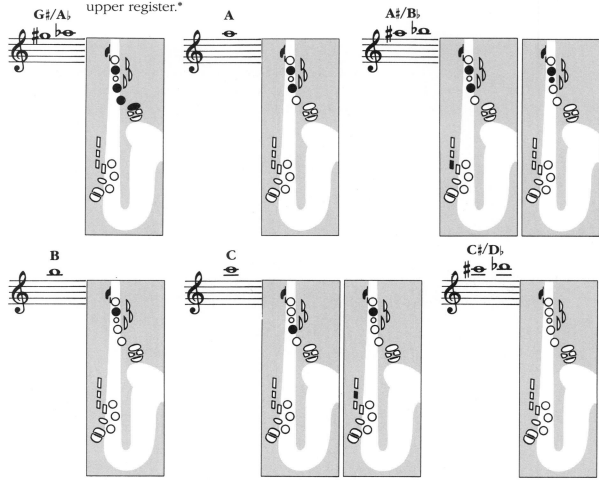

Intonation

Good **intonation**, or playing in tune, becomes critical in the upper register, particularly on the higher pitched saxophones such as the alto and soprano. The exercise for slurring octaves (p. 41) is designed to develop good intonation and a clear, effortless sound in the upper register.

It is important to tongue only the first note when playing these exercises. Keep the embouchure still, resisting any temptation to tighten up. It should be enough simply to provide a slight increase in support from the abdominal muscles. If the note stays in the upper register when you take the thumb off the octave key it probably means that you

*Many modern saxophones have a high F♯ key. The range can be further extended, by an octave or more depending on the skill of the player, by the use of **harmonics**, which involve an advanced blowing technique and special fingerings. Brass instruments like the trumpet work on a similar overblowing principle. It is not within the scope of this book to deal with harmonics, but the bibliography lists the best books on the subject.

tightened the embouchure when moving to the higher note. If the upper note is flat it may be that you are not sufficiently supporting the air column. If the problem persists try a harder reed.

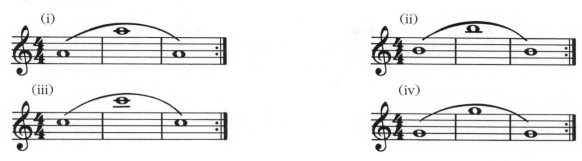

'Apologies To Daisy' was specially written for this book by the British Jazz composer Steve Berry, (b. 1957) who lives in Blackburn. Steve is perhaps best known for his work with the innovative jazz orchestra Loose Tubes, which contributed greatly to the resurgence of interest in jazz in Britain during the late 1980s.

Apologies to Daisy

Steve Berry

The Way of All Things

Scale and arpeggio practice: A minor

CHAPTER 13

Even Quavers

In classical music quavers, or eighth-notes, are invariably given half the value of crotchets but in jazz they can be interpreted in different ways. This chapter will deal with the classical interpretation, sometimes referred to by jazz musicians as 'even quavers' or 'straight eighths'.

Single quavers are written thus: ♪ or ♩ .

Beams

When there are two or more quavers
they may be connected by a **beam**, e.g., ♫ or ♬ .

Perform the following exercise:

Quavers can also be counted in this way:

To perform the drumming exercise below sit on a chair with your feet on the floor and the palms of your hands resting on the top of your thighs. You should attempt it very slowly at first.

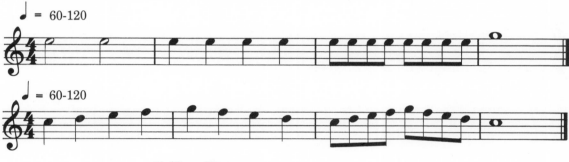

The next two exercises are to be played on the saxophone.

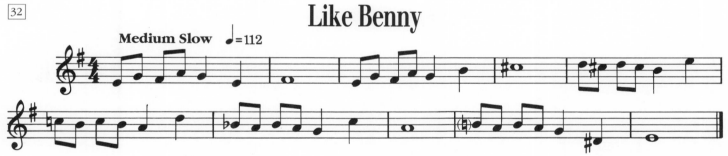

Like Benny

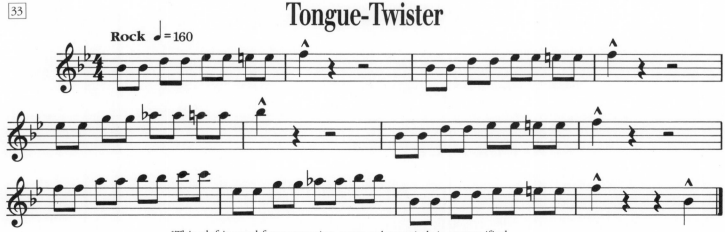

'Tongue-Twister' is an exercise for rapid tonguing. But do not strive for speed at the expense of even tone and rhythm. It is better to begin slowly and gradually increase the tempo, using a metronome if one is available.

Tongue-Twister

*This clef is used for percussion parts, where pitch is unspecified.

'Lullaby' was written by Californian pianist/composer Ted Gioia (b. 1957).* As well as making recordings under his own name he has worked with many fine musicians. He has taught jazz history and performance at Stanford University and is the author of two books on jazz, *The Imperfect Art* and *West Coast Jazz*.

Jazz-Rock

'Lullaby' is an example of a tune in a jazz-rock style. This style always calls for an even-quaver interpretation.

If you experience problems with the tied rhythm, e.g. in bars 2 and 3, try playing the phrase first **without** the tie. This will help you to see the correct placement of the notes.

D.C. al Fine

The direction *D.C. al Fine* is short for *Da Capo al Fine* (literally 'from the beginning to the end') and means repeat from the start of the piece and stop at the word *Fine*. **Rall.** is an abbreviation of *rallentando,* meaning 'getting slower'.

Lullaby
Ted Gioia

Scale and arpeggio practice: G major

E minor

FURTHER STUDY

Listening:
TED GIOIA, 'Lullaby in G' from *The End of the Open Road*.

*The original title is 'Lullaby in G'; this version is in C.

CHAPTER 14

Triplet Quavers

Triplet quavers occur when a crotchet beat is subdivided into three. They are notated like this:

Perform the following exercise:

One way of counting this rhythm is:

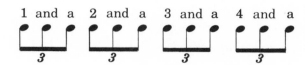

Drumming exercise

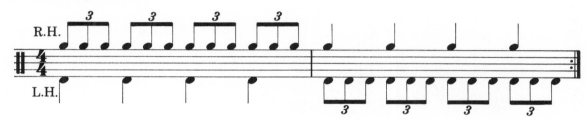

This exercise for rhythm and articulation would make an ideal daily warm-up, and should be practised on different notes throughout the saxophone range:

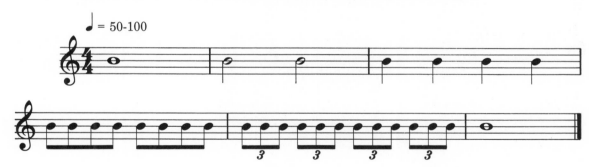

'Alicante' has a distinctly Spanish mood. Spanish music has inspired such famous musicians as Gil Evans, Miles Davis and Chick Corea.

Alicante

36

Exercise in Rhythm

Medium Swing ♩= 132
1.
2.
Fine
D.S. al Fine
without repeat

Thelonious Monk

'The Loneliest Monk' is dedicated to the late Thelonious Monk, a pianist and composer whose extraordinary originality was coupled with a wry humour. Together with Charlie Parker, Dizzy Gillespie, Bud Powell, Kenny Clarke and Max Roach, he created the explosive style of music called Bebop which dominated jazz during the 1940s and the early 1950s.

37

The Loneliest Monk

Slow Blues ♩= 86

Scale and arpeggio practice: B♭ major

G minor

FURTHER STUDY

Listening:

MILES DAVIS with the GIL EVANS ORCHESTRA, *Sketches of Spain*.
MILES DAVIS SEXTET, 'Flamenco Sketches' from *Kind of Blue*.
CHICK COREA, 'Spain', 'Señor Mouse', and 'Armando's Rhumba' from *Chick Corea*.

CHAPTER 15

This chapter deals with quavers which are played with a 'swing' rather than with even interpretation.

Swing Quavers

It is important to understand that there is no **visual** distinction between swing (or 'jazz') quavers and even quavers. The notes are written the same way but interpreted differently, the on-beat quaver having a value of two thirds of a beat and the off-beat quaver one third of a beat. Swing quavers are therefore closely related to triplet quavers:

but to notate them as they are played would be untidy and unnecessarily complicated.

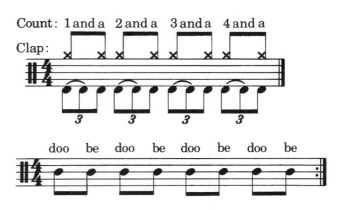

Practise the following exercise:

Scat-singing (see Chapter 11, p. 39) is an excellent way of establishing the correct 'feel' for jazz rhythms. One way of scatting jazz quavers is:

There are many other possibilities. Try inventing your own sounds. When the off-beat quaver is followed by silence, as in "Trane Refrain' I prefer a more emphatic scat-sound:

To Swing Or Not To Swing?

You may be wondering how you are to know whether the quavers should be played 'straight' or 'swung'. In many cases this is indicated by the expression markings at the beginning of the piece. Sometimes the composer/arranger specifically requests the desired quaver interpretation. In other cases the idiom dictates what is required. For example, if the piece is marked 'jazz-rock', 'latin', 'bossa-nova' or 'calypso' the quavers are played even, but 'swing', or 'medium blues' indicates jazz quavers.* If in doubt, try both ways and make an artistic choice!

With jazz quavers a little extra emphasis is generally given to the off-beat quaver. To achieve this jazz musicians often slur from off-beat to on-beat. Tonguing all the on-beats can make the music sound laboured. In order to practise this kind of phrasing scales should be played as follows:

Round and Round Again

---
*At fast tempos, even in music in a swing idiom, the quavers are played straight, since a smooth swing interpretation is impossible to achieve.

''Trane Refrain' is an example of the minor blues form which was often used by John Coltrane (1926-1967), who has inspired many musicians to take up the saxophone. His sound and style continue to exert a powerful influence on contemporary saxophone playing.

John Coltrane

Anticipation

When an off-beat jazz quaver is followed by a rest, as in the first six bars, or when it is tied over, as in the final six bars, it is often easier **not** to count the on-beat which immediately follows. This is because the off-beat jazz quaver functions as an **anticipation** of the following beat. It can therefore feel rushed and uncomfortable to count the next beat, especially if the tempo is fast. Try to 'feel' this beat without consciously counting it.

'Trane Refrain

'Blue Monk' is one of Thelonious Monk's most celebrated compositions.

The Blues Scale/Passing Notes

In 'Blue Monk' there is a twelve-bar improvisation section. The suggested scale for improvisation is often referred to by jazz educators as the blues scale. It is similar to the minor pentatonic scale you used for 'Blue Jean' in Chapter 9 (see p. 32) but it has one extra note—the flattened fifth, which in this case is D♭. This note has a very strong blues feeling. It sounds extremely dissonant or restless when played by itself and is more often used by jazz musicians as a passing note or connecting note, as in bars 1 and 3 of the upper part.*

Blue Monk

Thelonious Monk

Improvise on this scale:

D.C. al Coda

CODA

Repetition

A key word to remember when improvising is **repetition**. Many beginner improvisers make the mistake of simply running up and down the scale rather aimlessly. Repetition of single notes in interesting rhythms is a good way of breaking this habit. Lester Young and Sonny Rollins provide masterly examples of how effective note repetition can be in a jazz solo. Equally important is the use of riffs (see Chapter 2, p. 19), for which you will find no better model than guitarist Charlie Christian. Experiment by inventing your own riffs on 'Blue Monk' using the given scale.

FURTHER STUDY

Listening: JOHN COLTRANE, 'Mr. P.C.' from *Giant Steps* as an example of a minor blues.
THELONIOUS MONK, 'Blue Monk' from *Greatest Hits* or *The Composer*
CHARLIE CHRISTIAN, *The Genius of the Electric Guitar*.

*A dissonant note or chord is one which is discordant to the ear and sounds restless or in need of resolution. It does not have any negative connotations. Indeed, music without dissonance would be extremely dull.

CHAPTER 16

Off-Beat Phrases

So far all the phrases which you have played have started on the beat. The pieces in this chapter feature phrases which begin **off** the beat.

To begin with you may find it helpful to indicate the position of every quaver by counting as follows:

When you play phrases which begin off the beat you will therefore be entering on the 'and'. The example below shows how this counting method could be applied to the first two bars of 'A Bossa for Betty'.

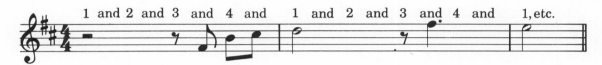

The symbol ⅞ is a quaver rest, worth half a beat. The note which follows it in the second bar is a dotted crotchet, worth one and a half beats. The off-beat dotted crotchet can therefore also be written:

A Bossa for Betty

'Familiarity' was written by British saxophonist and composer Pete Hurt (b. 1950), who has worked with George Russell and Carla Bley, and whose compositions have been played by—amongst others—the BBC Radio Big Band and the London Jazz Orchestra.

42

Familiarity

Pete Hurt

'Sister Caroline' features off-beat entries in a jazz-quaver context. Remember that an on-beat quaver rest is worth two thirds of a beat! The off-beat quaver is therefore later than when you are playing with an even-quaver interpretation. In order to achieve the correct interpretation listen to the CD and then try scatting what the saxophone is playing using the syllables written between the staves.

43

Sister Caroline

Scale and arpeggio practice: D major

B minor

CHAPTER 17

The Dotted Crotchet Followed By A Quaver

The new rhythm that you will meet in this chapter is the dotted crotchet followed by a quaver. The exercises below will help you to understand how this rhythm relates to previous rhythms you have learnt. They should be performed using both even- and jazz-quaver interpretations. It is particularly important that you count the beat immediately preceding the off-beat quaver.

N.B. (b) and (c), and (e) and (f) are identical rhythmically but notated differently.

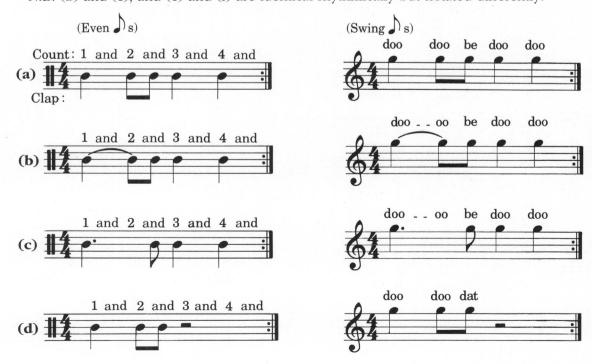

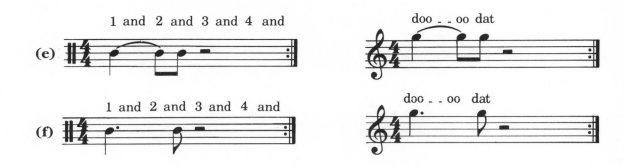

'Lucky Rhythm' was written by saxophonist/composer Tony Crowle (b. 1938), whose highly personal style has been a feature of the Oxford jazz scene for many years.

Lucky Rhythm

Tony Crowle

Summer Hummer

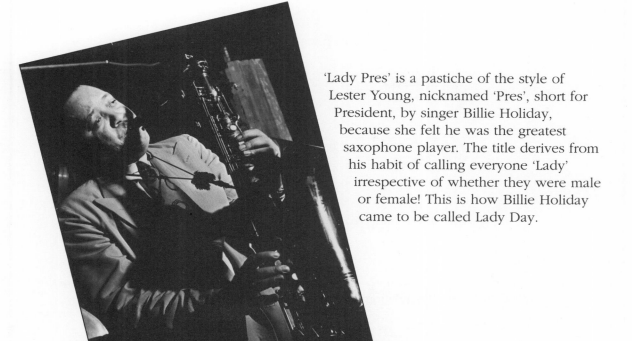

'Lady Pres' is a pastiche of the style of Lester Young, nicknamed 'Pres', short for President, by singer Billie Holiday, because she felt he was the greatest saxophone player. The title derives from his habit of calling everyone 'Lady' irrespective of whether they were male or female! This is how Billie Holiday came to be called Lady Day.

Lester Young

Lady Pres

Scale and arpeggio practice E♭ major

When playing the C minor arpeggio you will need to keep firm pressure with the little finger and slide from low C to E♭ using the rollers in between the two keys.

C minor

FURTHER STUDY

Listening:

LESTER YOUNG, 'Lady Be Good' from *The Essential Count Basie* Vol. 1.

Playing/Singing:

Listen to 'So What' from Miles Davis', *Kind of Blue*. The answering phrase played by the saxophones and trumpet in response to the bass figure is a dotted crotchet followed by a quaver, played with a swing feel. Try singing and then playing this phrase.

Reading:

LEWIS PORTER, *Lester Young*

CHAPTER 18

On-Beat Quaver Followed By Two Off-Beats

Another extremely common rhythm in jazz is the on-beat quaver followed by two consecutive off-beats. This may be encountered in various 'disguises' as will be apparent from the following exercises:

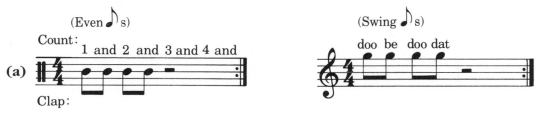

N.B. When clapped (b), (c), (d) and (e) sound the same, since the difference between them is only the *duration* of the notes and not their rhythmic position.

47

Country Road

Lazy Swing ♩=72

'Euphrates' was composed by Don Rendell (b. 1926), whose long career has included European tours with Stan Kenton and Woody Herman, work with Billie Holiday and many recordings and concert appearances with his own groups.

Modes

'Euphrates' is a **modal** piece. A **mode** is another name for a scale. Using the notes of each major scale it is possible to create six additional scales or modes by using each different degree of the scale as a start- and end-point. The scale which is produced by playing the notes of the C major scale from D to D is known as the **Dorian** mode:

This scale may be thought of as a variation of the minor scale since the first five notes are identical to those of the harmonic minor. It is the most commonly used mode in jazz. 'Euphrates' uses the modes of E Dorian (scale of D major starting on E) and F Dorian (scale of Eb major starting on F).

Ascending Melodic Minor Scale

This composition also introduces the **ascending melodic minor** scale. This is another variation of the minor scale in which the sixth note is raised by one semitone. Another way of thinking of it is as a major scale with the third note lowered one semitone.*

It is quite possible that you may get lost in your improvisation to begin with. If this happens try the following sequence of exercises:
1. Play the CD and count carefully through each eight-bar section.
2. Play a solo in semibreves only—one note to each bar. This will give you time to count the bars.
3. Play a solo using only minims.
4. Play a solo using only crotchets.

Practising in this way will help to develop your 'internal clock' which measures the passing of time in music. Eventually you will be able to 'feel' a two-, four- or eight-bar phrase without actually counting it.

*Classical musicians use a different form of the melodic minor scale in which the sixth and seventh notes are lowered by a semitone as it descends, i.e.:

Jazz musicians prefer to use the notes of the ascending form whether the scale is played rising or falling, hence the name by which it is known.

Euphrates

Don Rendell

Saxophone Section of the Count Basie Band (1970s)

'Endless Night' is the first example of the tango, a passionate Argentinian dance-form. Like other South American dances it requires an even-quaver interpretation

Endless Night

Tango ♩ = 120 (Even ♪s)

D.S. al Coda

CODA

FURTHER STUDY

Listening:

MILES DAVIS, *Kind of Blue*. This recording was one of the first to explore modal improvisation.

CHAPTER 19

The High Register

The notes at the top of the range present a considerable technical challenge. The keys are depressed not by the fingertips but by the inner part of the left hand, hence the expression 'palm-keys'. You are bound to find this a little awkward at first but do not be discouraged.

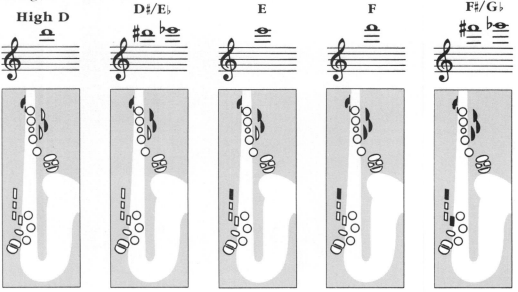

The following finger exercises should be played slowly, with full tone and even rhythm. The illustrations will show you which part of the hand should be used (see Figs. 29-33). Exercises involving high F♯ should only be played if you have a high F♯ key on your saxophone.*

Fig. 29 *Technique for high D*

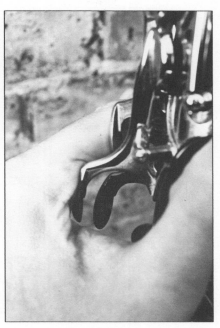

Fig. 30 *Left-hand technique for high E♭ and E*

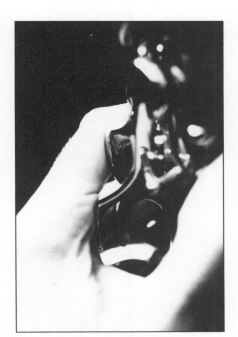

Fig. 31 *Left-hand technique for high F and F♯*

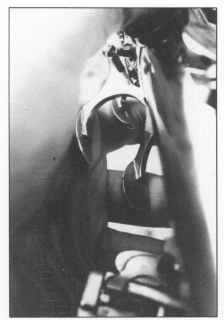

Fig. 32 *Technique for high F and F♯ showing points of contact from inside the hand*

Fig. 33 *Position of right hand for high E, F and F♯*

*High F♯ can still be played on saxophones which do not have a high F♯ key, by means of harmonics (see footnote to Chapter 12, p. 40).

Each exercise should be played several times.

If the instrument seems to be pushed over to the right by the movement of your left hand you are probably forgetting the importance of the slight forward push of the left thumb (see Part One: 'Posture', p. 7).

Remember not to tighten the embouchure for the high notes. Keep the throat open and relaxed and support the air column with the abdominal muscles.

The following is an unconventional ballad arrangement of a very familiar song.

2/2 Or Cut Time

This piece is written in 2/2 time. You should count two minim beats to a bar. This will mean that all notes and rests will get half their value in 4/4 time, e.g., a crotchet is only worth half a beat. Sometimes this time signature is written ¢ meaning cut time.

50

Oh When the Saints Go Marching In

Traditional arranged
by John O'Neill

Ballad ♩ =60

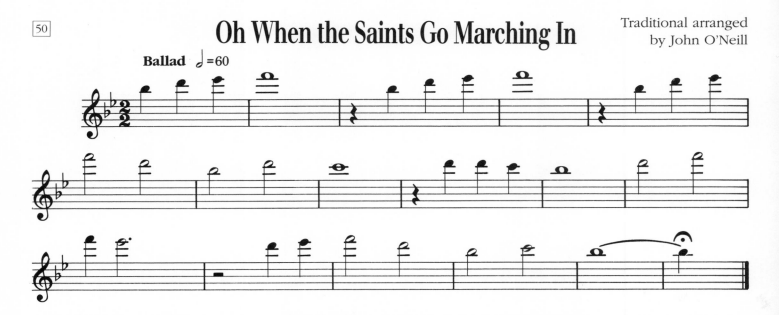

I Never Knew

Ted Gioia

Jazz Waltz ♩=144 (Swing ♪s)

FURTHER STUDY

Playing:

For additional high note practice, all of the tunes from Chapter 5 (pp. 26 & 27) and 'Romancing' from Chapter 8 (p. 31) should be played an octave higher. If your saxophone has a high F♯ you should similarly transpose the second version of 'Bird Waltz' from Chapter 10 (p. 35).

Play the chromatic scale over two octaves up and down from low F to high F.

Listening:

TED GIOIA/MARK LEWIS, 'I Never Knew' from *Tango Cool*.

CHAPTER 20

Low Notes

It is particularly difficult to play in the lowest register of the saxophone—the vibrating column of air has to be that much longer and the fingerings for the notes below bottom D are awkward. As if all this were not enough, tiny leaks higher up the instrument can make the very lowest tones difficult to produce except by resorting to excessive finger pressure, so make sure your instrument has been tested and found to be leak-free by a teacher or professional player before proceeding further. A reed which is too hard will also contribute to difficulties at the bottom end.

Certain saxophones do not play well in the lowest register even when they are in correct adjustment. If you experience this problem try putting two or three wine corks down the bell of the instrument. This was a tip given by Edward Planas, a leading expert on woodwind acoustics, and it can sometimes produce remarkable improvements.

To move between these new notes you will need to maintain firm pressure with the little finger and slide from one key to the other using the rollers (see Figs. 34, 35 and 36).

 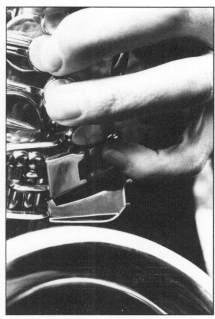 

Fig. 34 *Technique for low B*   Fig. 35 *Technique for low C♯*   Fig. 36 *Technique for bottom B♭*

You will probably find the exercises quite tiring, especially for the overworked left-hand little finger, so do not spend too much time on them in one practice session—a few minutes at the beginning will suffice.

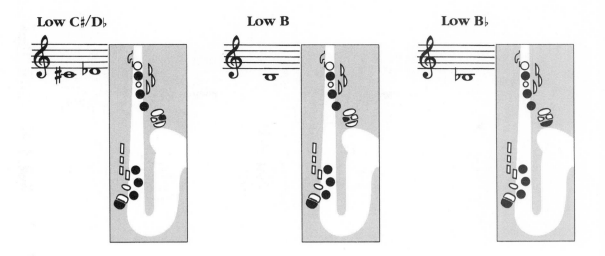

Low C♯/D♭   **Low B**   **Low B♭**

Each exercise should be played several times.

'Danny Boy', also known as the 'Londonderry Air' is a traditional Irish tune which has attracted many jazz musicians, including Ben Webster and Bill Evans.

52

Danny Boy

Traditional arranged by
John O'Neill and Phil Lee

Fall '90

FURTHER STUDY

Playing:

Play 'Oh When the Saints Go Marching In' (Chapter 19, p. 62) two octaves lower.

Play the chromatic scale over two octaves up and down from bottom B♭ to high B♭.

Listening:

BEN WEBSTER, 'Danny Boy' from *King of the Tenors*.

Ben Webster

CHAPTER 21

Construction Of Major And Minor Scales

The illustration below shows the distances between the component notes of the scale of C major, measured in tones and semitones. Semitones have already been discussed (see Chapter 4, p. 23). A tone is equal to two semitones. Do not be confused by the word tone. It has three possible meanings:

1. A means of expressing a particular distance between one note and another—as in the previous paragraph.
2. Sound, with special reference to quality, e.g. 'You have been trying to achieve a good **tone** on the saxophone'.
3. In American usage 'tone' is synonymous with the 'note', e.g. 'Play the first three **tones** of the C major scale'.

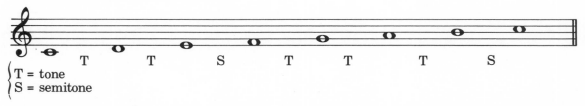

T = tone
S = semitone

Although the number of sharps or flats is different for every major scale the interrelationship of the notes is always the same. The sequence is always T T S T T T S.

For harmonic minor scales the sequence is as follows:

Notice the interval of a tone plus a semitone between the sixth and seventh degrees, which gives the scale its exotic 'Middle Eastern' quality.

Interrelationship Of Major And Minor Scales

The diagram on p. 68 will help you to understand how the major and minor scales relate to one another.

It is called a cycle of fourths/fifths because the distance between each scale and the next one in the cycle is a perfect fifth if measured downwards and a perfect fourth if measured upwards.*

It is important to note the following points about the cycle:

1. The direction of movement is **clockwise**, following a fundamental tendency of chords to move by intervals of a fourth upwards or a fifth downwards.
2. It is a cycle of increasing 'flatness' or decreasing 'sharpness', proceeding from one to seven flats, and from seven to one sharps.
3. Each major scale contains only one altered note in comparison with the previous scale in the cycle. This is the fourth note of the new scale, which is flattened by one semitone. For example, the only difference between C and F major is the B♭.
4. Sharps and flats cannot be mixed in the key signature.
5. Each harmonic minor scale contains the same notes as its relative major except for the seventh note which is raised by one semitone. The seventh note of both major and minor scales is often referred to as the **leading note** because of its tendency to lead back to the key note.

*For more information on intervals see the section on 'Ear Training', p. 37.

Cycle of 4ths/5ths

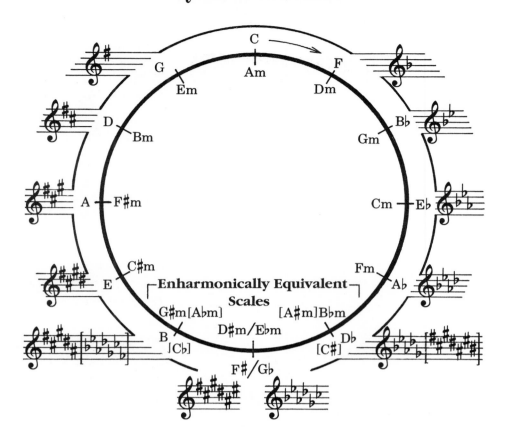

Enharmonic Scales

Notice the three enharmonic scales. Each of these scales can be thought of in two different ways (see Chapter 8, p. 31). The example below illustrates this. The scales are written differently but sound the same.

Practising The Scales

You should start with the C major and A minor scales and arpeggios and proceed through the cycle.

Now you have extended your range upwards and downwards you should practise the scales over the entire range and not simply from keynote to keynote. Saxophone technique is more difficult at the extremes of the instrument, so it is essential that you practise in these registers constantly, otherwise your effective range will be limited. A hallmark of the great saxophone players like Lester Young, Stan Getz, Sonny Rollins, Lee Konitz and John Coltrane is their ability to play over the entire range of the instrument (and sometimes beyond!).

Start on the lowest available key-note, play up to the highest note in that scale on your instrument, down to the lowest note in the scale and then back up to finish where you started. The example below shows how this would apply to the A major scale and arpeggio.

Scale Variations

I would suggest practising each scale with its relative minor and their arpeggios regularly for at least at week. Once you have mastered the basic scale you should start to practise variations. Below are just two examples in the key of C major:

You should also experiment with many different rhythms and articulations. The possibilities are endless. The complaint that scales are boring only comes from the unimaginative! If you want to learn to improvise you must learn to be creative in your practice.

Alternative High E, F and F♯

You should experiment with the alternative fingerings for high E, F and F♯ (see Figs. 37 and 38). You will find them particularly useful when moving from high C or C♯/D♭. At first you may find these notes a little more difficult to produce than the side fingerings, but it is worth persevering for the technical advantages which they offer.

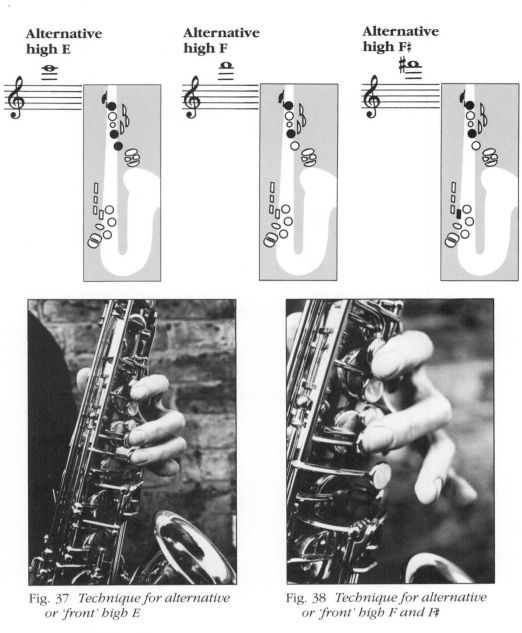

Alternative high E

Alternative high F

Alternative high F♯

Fig. 37 *Technique for alternative or 'front' high E*

Fig. 38 *Technique for alternative or 'front' high F and F♯*

FURTHER STUDY
Playing:
SIGURD RASCHER, *Scales For Saxophone*. This book explores the subject in a particularly imaginative way.

CHAPTER 22

Consecutive Off-Beats

You are already familiar with rhythms which involve two consecutive off-beats (Chapter 18, p. 56), but it is not uncommon to find a whole string of them. When playing even quavers consecutive off-beats can be counted as follows:

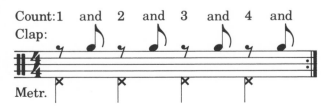

With jazz quavers counting becomes more problematic. At slow tempos you could adopt the following approach:

Scat:(doo) be (doo) be (doo) be (doo) be

Clap:

Metr.

However, at faster tempos there is no space to count the on-beat (see Chapter 15: Anticipation, p. 49) and you will have to rely on developing the correct 'feel'.

Perform the previous exercise setting the metronome at about 80 beats per minute and gradually increasing the tempo to 160.

You will probably notice one of two tendencies as the tempo increases: either the off-beat quaver becomes even rather than swung, which is a sign of rushing or playing ahead of the beat, or the off-beat gets closer and closer to the following beat, which is symptomatic of playing late or behind the beat. You will also notice a point where to say the 'doo' begins to feel uncomfortable and rushed so dispense with vocalizing the on-beat and try to feel the rhythm.

'Blue Samba' is a composition by Lee Konitz (b. 1926), who started his professional career in the band of Claude Thornhill and, after studying with Lennie Tristano, developed into one of the most individual voices of the alto saxophone and one of the most creative improvisors in jazz. Lee requested that this tune be written in fifteen keys (including the three enharmonic keys). That would be an interesting project for you!

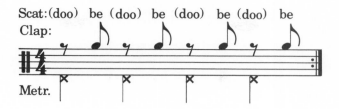

Lee Konitz

You will see that dots are written above or below some of the notes. Such notes are to be played **staccato**, or short and detached, but not accented.

Blue Samba

54

Lee Konitz

'Doxy' was written by Sonny Rollins (b. 1929), who established himself in the band led by drummer Max Roach and trumpeter Clifford Brown and whose unmistakable tone, and unique sense of phrasing and rhythm, make him one of the greatest tenor saxophone players in jazz.

55

Doxy

Sonny Rollins

'St Thomas' is a calypso, a dance form which originated in Trinidad. The calypso has a strong 'two-in-the-bar' feeling (see Chapter 19, p. 62). When you are learning the piece you may find it easier to count four in the bar, but you should aim to be able to count it in two.

56

St Thomas

Sonny Rollins

'The Right Time' is a composition by Dave Cliff (b. 1944), a jazz guitarist from Newcastle who has lived and worked in London for many years. He has played with a long list of great musicians, including Lee Konitz and Warne Marsh, and has received international recognition as a player whose rhythmic vitality extends the tradition of legendary guitarists Charlie Christian and Wes Montgomery.

57

The Right Time

Dave Cliff

FURTHER STUDY

Listening:

LEE KONITZ, 'Blue Samba' from *Zounds*

SONNY ROLLINS, 'Doxy' from *Prestige Years Vol. 2*. 'St. Thomas' from *Tenor Madness/Saxophone Colossus*.

DAVE CLIFF, 'The Right Time' from *The Right Time*.

CHAPTER 23

Triplet Crotchets

Triplet crotchets are exactly twice the length of triplet quavers and therefore involve grouping three notes against two beats. The following clapping exercise will help you to understand the relationship between triplet quavers and triplet crotchets:

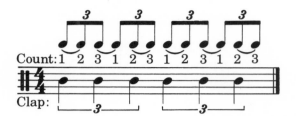

Once you have mastered the above try this exercise for tapping triplet crotchets against regular crotchets:

The triplet quavers have been written to enable you to work out the rhythm mathematically, but you should aim at being able to count the crotchet pulse and 'feel' the triplet crotchet rhythm.

Triplet crotchets should be played absolutely evenly—a common fault is to play the second one early and the third one late so that the rhythm resembles ♪♩ ♪ rather than ┌─3─┐ ♩ ♩ ♩.

The final section of 'Tango Cool' will give you a good opportunity to differentiate these two rhythms.

Tango Cool

Ted Gioia

Nicole

Dave Cliff

'Peace' was written by Horace Silver, who first received public acclaim as a member of Miles Davis' rhythm section of the early 1950s and later became famous as a composer and bandleader in his own right.

Peace

Horace Silver

FURTHER STUDY

Listening:

TED GIOIA/MARK LEWIS, 'Tango Cool' from *Tango Cool*.
DAVE CLIFF, 'Nicole' from *The Right Time*.
HORACE SILVER, 'Peace' from *Blowin' the Blues Away*.

CHAPTER 24

Harmony

Up until now your attempts at improvisation have been confined to different scales or modes. In order to become a complete musician you will also have to study **harmony**. Harmony is concerned with *simultaneous* sounds. It is one of the three great building blocks of music—the others being **rhythm**, or the organisation of notes in time, and **melody**, which deals with the ordering of *successive* sounds. It is not the intention of this book to deal with harmony in depth but rather to whet your appetite.

In Chapter 7 you were introduced to the idea of a triad. You can form a triad by taking any note of any major or minor scale and adding diatonic notes at intervals of a third.* Observe that the notes will either all be written on lines or all on spaces:

This procedure of building chords by stacking up notes in thirds can be extended to as many as seven notes, in which case all the notes in the scale are being played simultaneously. The example below shows a rearrangement of the notes of the C major scale.

If you have access to a piano and rudimentary knowledge of the keyboard you will benefit by exploring some of these exotic possibilities. If not, you should consider taking up the keyboard as a second study. Many jazz musicians have found that knowledge of the keyboard opens up exciting new possibilities in improvisation. Dizzy Gillespie, Bob Brookmeyer and Gerry Mulligan are just three famous examples.

Diatonic Chords

In modern jazz the four-note chord (with added seventh) is the basic unit of harmony. It is therefore important for you to get to know the diatonic four-note chords in each major and harmonic minor scale. Below are examples for the keys of G major and E minor.

---

*Diatonic notes are those which belong to the scale in question.

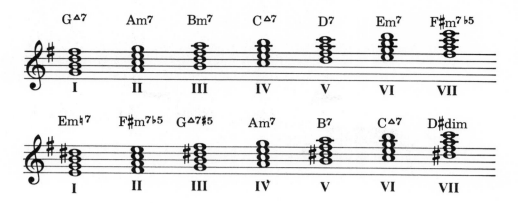

Chord Symbols

Below each chord is a Roman numeral which identifies the scale degree on which it is based. Written above each chord is a **chord symbol**, which is a kind of harmonic shorthand used by jazz musicians to identify different chord types. You need not know all of these at present. The following are the most important:

△7 = major seventh (major triad + major seventh measured from lowest note)
7 = seventh (major triad + minor seventh)
m7 = minor seventh (minor triad + minor seventh)
m7♭5 = minor seventh with a flattened fifth*

Below is the chord progression to the tune 'Fall '90' from Chapter 20, p. 66.

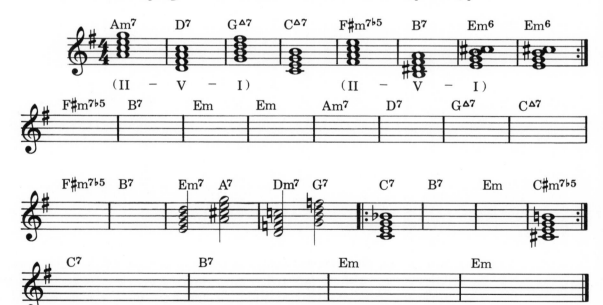

If you look at the direction of movement or **resolution** of the chords you will see that much of the time it follows the direction of the cycles of fourth/fifths (p. 68).

II-V-I Progression

You will see that the harmony of this tune largely consists of movement from the II chord to the V chord to the I chord in the keys of G major and E minor.** This is the **II-V-I progression**, by far the most common chord progression in jazz.

*This chord is indicated by some jazz educators with the symbol Ø.
**The Em6 chord (E-G-B-C♯) has been substituted for the Em♮7 but its harmonic function is the same.

The following sequence of exercises will help to familiarize you with the chord progression of 'Fall '90'. It may take you a long time to master them, but please persevere—the knowledge you gain will sharpen your ear and help your improvisation to become more sophisticated. A similar sequence of exercises could be used for learning the harmony of any standard tune.

N.B. Chords are written for reference only. All the exercises should be memorized and played by ear.

Chord Roots

● Sing and then play the **root** progression. The root is the scale degree on which the chord is built. There are different ways of performing this exercise, since you have a choice of whether you move up or down to the next note. Example:

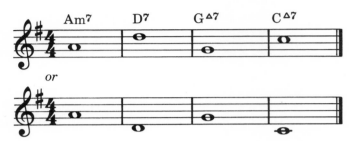

● Sing and play the chord progression, one note to each beat. Example:

N.B. For the bars with two chords you should play just the root and the third, e.g.:

The arpeggios can also be played descending, e.g.:

Voice-Leading

● Improvise a melodic line in semibreves, using chord notes only. This is an excellent exercise for **voice-leading,** or the smooth connection of one chord with another. It is usually better to move from one chord to the next by moving in small steps, although bigger intervals can be used for dramatic effect. Feel free to repeat notes if they are common to both chords. Example:

● Improvise a line in minims, using chord notes only. Example:

- Improvise in crotchets using chord notes only. This is closely related to the 'walking bass' technique used by jazz bass players. You may need to make room for breathing spaces, by leaving out notes here and there. Example:

- Improvise in free rhythm using chord notes only. Example:

- Improvise freely using additional notes from the C major and A minor scales and any others which sound good!

FURTHER STUDY

Playing:

JERRY COKER, *Jerry Coker's Jazz Keyboard*. An excellent book for developing jazz keyboard skills, for pianists and non-pianists.

LIONEL GRIGSON, *Practical Jazz*. A thorough exploration of jazz harmony and its relevance for improvisation.

CHAPTER 25

Semiquavers

Semiquavers, or sixteenth notes, are half the length of even quavers. Rhythms which involve semiquavers can look very complicated—suddenly the manuscript becomes very black!—but try not to be intimidated. If you look carefully at the rhythm exercises on p. 80 you will see that the mathematical relationship between the notes in the semiquaver examples in 2/4 is the same as in the quaver examples in 4/4 which are written next to them. It is only the unit of time that you are counting which changes.

For this reason you may initially find it helpful to count the quaver beat when playing semiquaver rhythms. This means that the first example would be counted as follows:

Another option would be to count like this:

You could apply the same principle to the other exercises, but work towards being able to count crotchet beats.

The sign ꓶ is a semiquaver rest.

Drumming Exercise

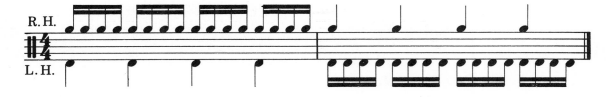

The following exercise will provide excellent practice both for rhythm and articulation. It should be played for a few minutes at each practice session as part of your warm-up until you have mastered it:

Spanish Steps

[61]

'Persuasion' was written by American pianist/composer Roland Perrin (b. 1959), who is based in London. He has played with Dudu Pukwanu and The Brotherhood Of Breath and is currently the composer/arranger/bandleader of the group Evidence. His musical influences include African and South American music, Duke Ellington and Mahler!

Persuasion

Roland Perrin

[62]

Grace Notes

The F# written before the G in bars 12 and 15 of 'It's All Yours' is a **grace note**. It should be played on the beat and 'crushed' against the note which follows. Try to imitate the example on the CD.

On the Street

Since the early 1960s there has been increasing experimentation with time signatures other than 3/4 or 4/4 in jazz. Pianist Dave Brubeck and trumpeter Don Ellis were among the first to experiment widely with unusual time signatures.

6/8 Time

6/8 time means that you count six quavers to a bar, although at faster tempos this is nearly always counted in two (dotted-crotchet beats), with each beat subdivided into three. The exercises below show both possibilities for counting.

Paul Desmond

'Greensleeves' is an old English tune which can be traced back at least as far as the sixteenth century and has sometimes been attributed to Henry VIII. It has attracted the attention of many jazz musicians, including John Coltrane and Paul Desmond, probably because of its modal nature.

65

Greensleeves

Traditional arranged by Phil Lee

5/4 Time

Like many of the more complex time signatures, such as 7/4 or 11/4, 5/4 is nearly always subdivided into a combination of two- and three-beat groupings. You will probably find it easier to count these groups of two or three rather than the actual number of beats in the bar. In 'Five Jive' the subdivision is three followed by two.

Irregular Phrasing

Irregular phrasing occurs when a phrase is repeated in unpredictable positions within the bar. In 'Straight, No Chaser' the phrasing is completely asymmetrical, making it very difficult to know where the 'one' is. Careful counting is the only solution.

FURTHER STUDY

Listening:

PAUL DESMOND, 'Greensleeves' from *East of the Sun*.

JOHN COLTRANE, 'Greensleeves' from *Africa Brass*.

CHARLES MINGUS, 'Better Git It In Your Soul' from *Mingus Ah Um*. Another example of 6/8 time.

DAVE BRUBECK, *Time Out*. Features Paul Desmond's composition 'Take Five', one of the most famous tunes in an unusual time signature.

Playing:

LOESBERG, JOHN, ed., *An Irish Tunebook*. Parts One and Two. The books contain much immensely enjoyable and exciting music in 6/8 time. They also provide excellent practice for technique, rhythm and articulation and good source material for learning by heart and transposition.

CODA

No book on saxophone playing would be complete without including something by Charlie Parker, whose musical personality has had such an enormous influence on jazz and twentieth-century music in general. His life and music have been the subject of a film and several books (see bibliography to Chapter 11). Enjoy these two tunes, learn them by heart and let them become part of you.

My Little Suede Shoes

Charlie Parker

Yardbird Suite

Charlie Parker

FURTHER STUDY

Listening:

'My Little Suede Shoes' from *Charlie Parker*.

'Yardbird Suite' from *Bird Symbols*.

Charlie Parker

Part Three: Appendices

BIBLIOGRAPHY

The following publications are those to which specific reference is made in the sections entitled Further Study.

COKER, JERRY. *Jerry Coker's Jazz Keyboard* (Florida, Colombia Pictures Publications, 1984)

GIDDINS, GARRY. *Celebrating Bird: The Triumph of Charlie Parker.* (New York, Beech Tree Books, William Morrow and Company, Inc., 1987)

GRIGSON, LIONEL. *Practical Jazz* (London, Stainer and Bell, 1988)

HINDEMITH, PAUL. *Elementary Training for Musicians* (London, Schott, 1946)

LOESBERG, JOHN Ed. *An Irish Tunebook* Parts One and Two (Cork, Ossian Publications, 1986)

PORTER, LEWIS. *Lester Young* (London, MacMillan Press, 1985)

RASCHER, SIGURD. *Scales for Saxophones* (New York, McGinnis and Marx, 1965)

REISNER, ROBERT. *Bird: The Legend of Charlie Parker* (New York, Citadel Press, 1962)

RUSSELL, ROSS. *Bird Lives* (New York, Charterhouse, 1973)

TEAL, LARRY. *The Art Of Saxophone Playing* (Evanston, Illinois, Summy-Birchard Company, 1963)

These books are recommended for general background and interest:

GIOIA, TED. *The Imperfect Art* (New York, Oxford University Press, 1988). A unique and thought-provoking discussion on the place of jazz in modern culture.

GRIME, KITTY. *Jazz at Ronnie Scott's* (London, Robert Hale, 1979). A fascinating collection of anecdotes and aphorisms by musicians who have played at the club.

HENTOFF, NAT and NAT SHAPIRO. *Hear Me Takin' to Ya: The Story of Jazz by the Men Who Made It* (New York, Rinehart, 1955). Complements perfectly the Kitty Grime book noted above.

KERNFELD, BARRY ed. *The New Grove Dictionary of Jazz* (London, Macmillan Press, 1988). A significant investment but worth every penny. The most complete and authoritative reference work on the subject.

The books below are recommended for developing technique, musicianship and improvisational skills:

BACH, J.S. *15 Two-part Inventions*, ed. Larry Teal, adapted for saxophone duet—2 E♭ alto saxophones or one E♭ alto and one B♭ tenor saxophone. (Bryn Mawr, Pennsylvania; Theodore Presser Company, 1969.) Beautiful examples of melodic invention which will develop sure technique.

RAE, JAMES. *20 Modern Studies for Solo Saxophone* (London, Universal Edition, 1989). Especially good for further practice of unusual and changing time signatures.

RASCHER, SIGURD M. *158 Saxophone Exercises* (Copenhagen, Wilhelm Hansen, 1968). Complements *Scales for Saxophone* by the same author and has an equally imaginative approach. Used by John Coltrane, if further recommendation were needed!

—*Top-tones for the Saxophone* (New York, Carl Fischer Inc., 1941). A masterly exploration of the subject of harmonics and the extended range.

ROUSSEAU, EUGENE. *Saxophone High Tones* (Bloomington, Indiana; Étoile Music, 1978). Complements Rascher's *Top-tones*. The fingering charts are excellent.

SHANAPHY ED. and STUART ISACOFF. *Dick Hyman's Professional Chord Changes and Substitutions For 100 Tunes Every Musician Should Know* (New York, Ekay Music, 1986). Valuable for building a repertoire of tunes. The melodies and chords are accurate and there is the added bonus of lyrics, which are indispensable for learning how to phrase a tune properly.

TELEMANN, GEORGE PHILIPP. *Six Canonic Sonatas* arranged for two saxophones by Larry Teal. (Bloomington, Indiana, Étoile Music, 1978.) Excellent studies for developing listening skills as well as technique.

VIOLA, JOSEPH. *The Technique of the Saxophone Vol. 3: Rhythm Studies* (Boston, Berklee Press Publications, 1971). The little rhythmic studies for two saxophones in the first half of the book are particularly good for developing reading skills in the jazz idiom.

APPENDIX 2

DISCOGRAPHY

Every effort has been made to ensure that this discography is as up to date and accurate as possible at the time of writing but since recordings are being deleted and reissued all the time it is impossible to guarantee that all are currently available. Similarly, if a recording is not listed in the format you require, e.g. CD, record or cassette, you should not conclude that it is permanently unavailable in that format.

Should you find it difficult to obtain any of the recordings try looking in one of the many specialist jazz record shops, most of which have second-hand sections and also import recordings from other countries.

This discography was compiled with the expert assistance of Bob Glass of Ray's Jazz Shop Ltd, 180 Shaftesbury Avenue, London.

Key: CD = compact disc; LP = long-playing record; C = cassette

ADDERLEY, CANNONBALL. *Somethin' Else* (Blue Note CDP 7 46338 2 [CD])

ARMSTRONG, LOUIS. *Hot 5 and Hot 7 (1925-1928)* (Giants of Jazz GOJCD 53001)

BAKER, CHET. *The Touch of Your Lips* (Steeplechase SCS-1122 [LP])

BASIE, COUNT. *Swinging the Blues* (That's Jazz TJCD 0004 [CD] TJMC 0004 [C, LP])

—*The Essential Count Basie Vol. 1* (CBS 460061 1 [LP], 460061 2 [CD] 460 061 4 [C])

—*The Essential Count Basie Vol. 2* (CBS 460828 1 [LP], 460828 2 [CD], 460828 4 [C])

BRUBECK, DAVE. *Time Out* (CBS [Sony Music] 4606111 [LP], 4606112 [CD], 4604114 [C])

BYAS, DON with SLAM STEWART, TEDDY WILSON and FLIP PHILLIPS, *Town Hall Concert Vol. 3* in The Commodore Series (London HMC 5003 [LP])

CHRISTIAN, CHARLIE. *The Genius of the Electric Guitar* from the CBS Jazz Masterpieces series (CBS [Sony Music] 4606122 [CD], 4606121 [LP], 4606124 [C])

CLIFF, DAVE. *The Right Time* (Miles Music MM074 [LP])

COLTRANE, JOHN. *Giant Steps* (Atlantic [Warner Music UK Ltd] WEA 7567·81337·2 [CD], ATL 50239 or 50239 [LP])

—*Africa Brass* (Impulse [New Note] MCAD 42001 [CD])

—*A Love Supreme* (MCA DMCL 1648 [CD]. MCL 1648 [LP] MCLC 1648 [C])

COREA, CHICK. *Chick Corea* from the Compact Jazz and Walkman Jazz series (Polydor [Polygram] 8313652 [CD], 8313654 [C])

DAVIS, MILES. *Kind of Blue* (CBS [Sony Music] CD 62066 [CD], 62066 [LP])

—*Sketches of Spain* (CBS [Sony Music] 460 604 1/2/4 [LP, CD, C])

DESMOND, PAUL. *East of the Sun* (Discovery DSCD-840 [CD])

EVANS, BILL. *At the Village Vanguard* (OJC 140 [LP] OJC CD 140 [CD])

EVANS, GIL. *Gil Evans & 10* (Prestige DJC-346/P-7120 [LP]). Features soprano saxophonist Steve Lacey.

FITZGERALD, ELLA. *Sings the Duke Ellington Songbook* (Verve [Polygram] 8370352 [CD])

GETZ, STAN. *Focus* (Verve [Polygram] 8219822 [CD])

—*Jazz Samba* (Verve [Polydor] 8100611 [LP], 8100612 [CD], 8100614 [C])

—*Stan Getz and Joao Gilberto* (Verve [Polydor] 841 445 2/4 [CD, C])

—*Sweet Rain* (Verve 815 054-2 [CD])

—*Serenity* (Emarcy 838770-2 [CD])

GIOIA, TED. *The End of the Open Road* (Quartet Q-1001-CD [CD])

GIOIA, TED/MARK LEWIS, *Tango Cool* (Quartet QCD 1006 [CD])

GIUFFRE, JIMMY. *The Jimmy Giuffre 3* (Atlantic Jazz 7 90981-2 [CD])

GORDON, DEXTER. *At Montreux* (Prestige PCD 7861-2 [CD])

GRAY, WARDELL. (Wardell Gray Quintet.) *Live at the Haigh 1952* (Fresh Sound Records FSR CD 157 [CD])

HAWKINS, COLEMAN. *Hollywood Stampede* (Capitol Jazz CDP 7 92596 2 [CD])

HAWKINS, COLEMAN and LESTER YOUNG, *Classic Tenors* (Joker SM 3259 [LP])

HODGES, JOHNNY with DUKE ELLINGTON, *Side by Side* (Verve [Polydor] 8215782 [CD])

HODGES, JOHNNY with OLIVER NELSON and LEON THOMAS, *Three Shades of Blue* (RCA NL89710 [LP])

JARREAU, AL. *Breakin' Away* (Warner Bros 256917 [CD])

KONITZ, LEE. *Motion* (Verve [Polygram] 8215532 [CD])

—*Konitz Meets Mulligan* (Pacific Jazz [EMI] CZ 45/CDP 7468472 [CD], TCWP 6 [C])

—*I Concentrate On You* (Steeplechase SCCD-31018 [CD])

—*Zounds* (Soul Note SN 121-219-2 [CD])

MARSH, WARNE. *Star Highs* (Criss Cross CRISS 1002 [CD])

—*A Ballad Album* (Criss Cross CRISS 1007 [LP])

McFERRIN, BOBBY. *Spontaneous Inventions* (Blue Note CDP 7462982 [CD], BN2 57 [C], BT 85110 [LP])

MINGUS, CHARLES. *Mingus Ah-Um* (CBS [Sony Music] 4504361 [LP], 4504362 [CD], 4504364 [C])

MONK, THELONIOUS. *The Composer* from the Contemporary Jazz Masterpieces series (CBS [Sony Music] 463382 or CK 44297 [CD], 463 338 1/2/4 [LP, CD, C]) or CJT 44927 [C/LP])

MULLIGAN, GERRY. *Gerry Mulligan Concert Jazz Band* from the Compact Jazz Series (Verve 838 933-2 [CD])

—*The Age of Steam* from the Jazz Heritage series (A & M CDA 0804 [CD])

PARKER, CHARLIE. *Charlie Parker* in the Compact Jazz and Walkman Jazz series (Verve [Polygram] 8332882 [CD] 8332884 [C])

—*Bird Symbols* (Rhapsody [President] RHCD 5 [CD], RHAP 5 [LP])

—*The Best of Bird on Savoy* (Vogue 650109 [CD])

PEPPER, ART. *Gettin' Together* (Contemporary Records S7573 [LP])

ROLLINS, SONNY. *Prestige Years Vol. 2* (1954-1956) (Prestige PRE 4002 [CD])

—*Tenor Madness/Saxophone Colossus* (Prestige [Ace] CDJZD 002 [CD])

—*Way Out West Plus* (Contemporary [Ace] CDCOP 006 [CD] COP 006 [LP])

—*And The Contemporary Leaders* (Contemporary [Ace Records] CDCOP 018 [CD])

SHORTER, WAYNE. *Native Dancer* (CBS 4670952 [CD])

—*Atlantis* (CBS CDCBS 26669 [CD], CBS 26669 [LP])

SILVER, HORACE. *Blowin' the Blues Away* (Blue Note/EMI BN2 89/CDP 7465262 [CD], 4BN 84017 [C], BST 84017 [LP])

SIMS, ZOOT. *Warm Tenor* (Pablo 2310 831 [LP])

STEPS AHEAD, *Steps Ahead* (Elektra [Warner Music UK Ltd] 9601682 [CD]). Features tenor saxophonist Michael Brecker.

WEBSTER, BEN. *King of the Tenors* (Verve 837 437-1 [CD])

WEBSTER, BEN and SWEETS EDISON, *Ben and 'Sweets'* (CBS 4606131 [LP], 4606132 [CD], 4606134 [C])

WOODS, PHIL. *Live* (Novus [BMG Records Ltd] ND 83104 [CD])

Mention should also be made of the series of play-a-long CDs, records and cassettes produced by the American jazz educator **Jamey Aebersold**. There are, at the time of writing, 52 of these featuring compositions by great musicians and also many excellent 'standard' tunes. The records are suitable for either alto or tenor saxophone and come complete with a booklet which includes melody, chord-progressions and sometimes lyrics. The booklets also sometimes include helpful advice on improvisation. The recordings feature a rhythm section of bass, drums and piano which provides a backing track against which to play the tune   and then improvise. These rhythm sections are made up of professional jazz musicians, many of whom are among the finest players in the world. Vol. 2 *Nothin' But The Blues* and Vol. 5 *Time To Play Music* are particularly suitable for students moving on from this book.

MOUTHPIECES AND REEDS

When saxophone players get together they nearly always seem to end up talking about mouth-pieces! The mouthpiece certainly has a crucial effect on the tone-quality and ease of playing. The right mouthpiece on a student model instrument will invariably produce better results than the wrong one on an expensive saxophone. Let us consider the factors which have a major bearing on mouthpiece performance.

Tip opening

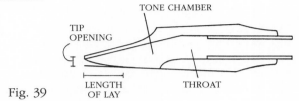

Fig. 39

The wider the opening, the more effort is required to make the reed vibrate, since it has further to travel. Wide tip openings usually require softer reeds, and narrow openings require harder reeds.

Length of lay

A longer lay will make for easier blowing, but if it is too long it may make tuning difficult to control.

Tone chamber

A bigger chamber produces a rounder sound, a smaller chamber a more brilliant sound.

Baffle

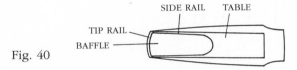

Fig. 40

The baffle is the slightly raised area near the mouthpiece tip. A high baffle will produce a more 'edgy' sound than a lower one. Many modern mouthpieces have a 'super-baffle' or step built into them for extra brilliance.

Rails

The rails should be straight and not much thicker than one millimetre at the thinnest point. Ultra-thin rails, however, are likely to encourage tonal instability and squeaks..

Throat

For jazz playing it is best if the throat is 'straight through'. Some classical mouthpieces have a square- or arch-shape cut into them.

The mouthpiece which comes with the instrument is rarely suitable. Such mouthpieces are often cheaply made, and the tip opening is usually too close or too open. It would be advisable to change to a better one at the earliest opportunity.

When purchasing a mouthpiece examine it carefully to see how well finished it is. It should be perfectly symmetrical. Check that the rails begin to curve at exactly the same point and that the table (Fig. 40) is completely flat. Be cautious. Many modern mouthpieces, even expensive ones, are poorly finished.

It is not advisable to spend too much money on your first mouthpiece, in case it should ultimately prove to be unsuitable. Metal mouthpieces are more expensive but they are not necessarily better. For alto players the Meyer represents extremely good value, and a tip opening of 5MM or 6MM would be suitable. For tenor players the ebonite Otto Link, either 6☆ or 7☆ is recommended.

Reeds

Even a good mouthpiece will produce poor results if the reed is of poor quality, the wrong grade or the incorrect strength. It is not within the scope of this book to discuss reeds in depth but the most pertinent factors are as follows:

Quality

Never use cheap reeds. Rico, La Voz, Vandoren and Olivieri are some of the better brand names.

Strength

Most reeds are numbered to indicate strength—the higher the number the harder the reed. La Voz are actually marked in five grades between soft and hard. Beware of making comparisons between different manufacturers, since grading systems vary. Beginners should generally use a medium-soft or medium reed (grades 2—2$^1/_2$) unless the mouthpiece tip-opening is very narrow, in which case the use of a harder reed may be warranted, or very wide, in which case you should use a softer reed.

If the reed is too soft the sound will tend to be feeble and reedy and the high notes will be flat and difficult to produce. Tonguing will also be more difficult, since the reed will have less spring in it.

If on the other hand the reed is too hard your sound will be very breathy; your supply of breath will quickly be exhausted and your embouchure will tire rapidly. The low notes will be particularly difficult to produce.

Purchase

You should take advantage of the fact that most shops will allow you to examine reeds before purchase. Look for a golden colour in the blade of the reed. White or green tinges mean that the cane was not mature when cut. Dark brown streaks are not a good sign. Hold the reed up to the light. You should reject any which are chipped or cracked. Examine the grain, which should run parallel with the sides of the reed. It is particularly important that the fibres in the centre run all the way to the tip.

FURTHER STUDY

Reading:

LARRY TEAL, *The Art of Saxophone Playing.*

USEFUL ACCESSORIES

Pull-Through

The best quality pull-throughs are usually chamois leather next to a brush attached to a long piece of weighted cord. This is dropped down the bell of the saxophone, which is then inverted, allowing the weight to fall out of the other end so that it can be pulled through. The purpose of the pull-through is to remove moisture from the pads and so prolong their life. Beware of the large mops which are currently marketed as an alternative. Although they can be used to clean the instrument out, they should not be left inside the saxophone, since this will not allow the pads to dry.

Reed Guard

This protects the reeds from being chipped and also keeps them flat and prevents warping.

Mouthpiece Patches

These are placed on top of the mouthpiece. They cushion the teeth against vibration, which is helpful if you have sensitive teeth but, even if you do not, they make the mouthpiece feel more comfortable and make it easier for you to achieve consistent placement of the teeth.

Set of Small Screwdrivers

The screws on saxophones are never over-tightened, and therefore even on the best instruments it is possible that they can work loose through playing. Examine your instrument carefully once a week and tighten any loose screws. *Do not over-tighten.*

Tuning Fork

It is best to obtain an A = 440 tuning fork, which corresponds to B on B♭ saxophones and F♯ on E♭ saxophones.

Metronome

Make sure the metronome clicks loudly enough to be heard. This tends to be more of a problem with electronic metronomes than with mechanical ones.

Cork Grease

The 'lip-salve' type containers are better, since they prevent the grease transferring to your fingers and then being deposited on the saxophone keys.

Reedcutter

A useful device for clipping a small amount off a reed which is too soft, thus making it playable.

Duster or Soft Cloth

For keeping the outside of the instrument clean.

Cotton Buds

For cleaning in those places where a duster cannot reach, e.g. under the rods and around the pillars.

Neck-Strap

Since most of the weight of the alto, tenor and baritone saxophones bears down on the neck it makes sense to have a good quality neck-strap. The strap should have a wide band, be easily adjustable, should not slip, and should preferably have a strong clip which does not allow the saxophone to unhook itself.

APPENDIX **5**

CARE OF THE INSTRUMENT

After you have finished playing use a pull-through to clean the instrument (this is not possible with the soprano or baritone), or insert and then remove the cleaning mop. You should remove the reed, **gently** wipe off excess moisture, and clean the inside of the mouthpiece with a tissue, taking great care not to rub too hard in the area of the baffle and mouthpiece tip.

Where possible you should brush your teeth before playing, especially if you have just eaten. Mouthpieces are an ideal breeding ground for bacteria. It is particularly important not to play immediately after consuming sweetened foods or drinks.

Cork-grease should be sparingly applied whenever the cork on the crook shows signs of drying out, otherwise it may crack and need replacing.

A duster can be used to remove marks from the lacquered body, and to keep the instrument shiny. Cotton buds can be used to reach awkward places.

It is inevitable that deposits will build up on the reed and affect reed performance. I recommend cleaning reeds with an old toothbrush in warm water, taking care to avoid passing the brush across the tip, and always brushing in the direction of the grain. Rinse the reeds in cold water.

Overhauls and repairs should be entrusted only to an experienced saxophone technician.

APPENDIX **6**

TRANSPOSITION

Saxophones are transposing instruments. In other words the note you play is not the note that actually sounds. When you play C, the note that sounds is concert pitch E♭ on E♭ saxophones and concert pitch B♭ on B♭ saxophones.

As long as you are playing by yourself or with other saxophones of the same pitch this will not make any difference, but in order to play with concert-pitch instruments like piano or guitar, or with instruments pitched in keys other than that of your own saxophone you must **transpose** your music into another key, or they must transpose into your key.

To transpose music written at concert pitch to the correct key for E♭ saxophones play a major sixth higher or, if this is beyond your working range, a minor third lower, which will produce the same pitch an octave lower.* For B♭ saxophones the transposition is up a tone and an octave, or up a tone if this places you too high in your range.

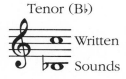

*See section on intervals in Chapter 11 (p. 37).

To transpose E♭ saxophone music to the B♭ saxophone play a fourth higher or a fifth lower. To transpose B♭ saxophone music to the E♭ saxophone play a fourth lower or a fifth higher.

When transposing it is important first to change the key signature, either mentally, if you are simply playing a tune written at concert pitch, or on paper, if you are trying to write it down. This will save you having to think of each note individually. Be careful, however, with accidentals, particularly when applied to the notes B and E. Remember, sharps and flats can transpose to naturals and vice versa. The examples below will illustrate the pitfalls.

SOME THOUGHTS ABOUT PRACTICE

Try to make the environment you practise in as pleasant as possible. The room should be bright and well ventilated. It should also preferably not be too cluttered—if there is a lack of bare wall space the room will lack resonance and your sound will be deadened. Soft furnishings like thick carpets and curtains have a particularly muffling effect. On the other hand this might be an advantage if your neighbours complain about the noise!

It is very important to practise regularly—every day if possible. Twenty minutes a day is much more valuable than one or two longer sessions a week. If you practise more intensively remember that it is more effective to play for short periods of twenty minutes to half an hour with breaks in between than to play for hours at a stretch.

Do not expect to progress at a uniform rate, however hard you practise. The foundation techniques in particular can take a long time to master. Very often you will encounter the 'plateau effect' where you feel for a long time that you are not progressing at all. Do not be discouraged! Such periods are nearly always followed by a dramatic leap forward.

● Avoid practising when you are tired. It may be more effective to practise at the beginning or middle of the day than at the end if your lifestyle permits.

● Do not practise in a half-hearted way—you will be wasting your time.

● Warm up properly—long notes or simple tonguing exercises are ideal.

● You can do a lot of valuable practice without the instrument in your hands—singing, clapping or listening to music for example.

● Avoid becoming obsessed by any one aspect of your playing—there are many different skills to acquire.

FINGERING CHART

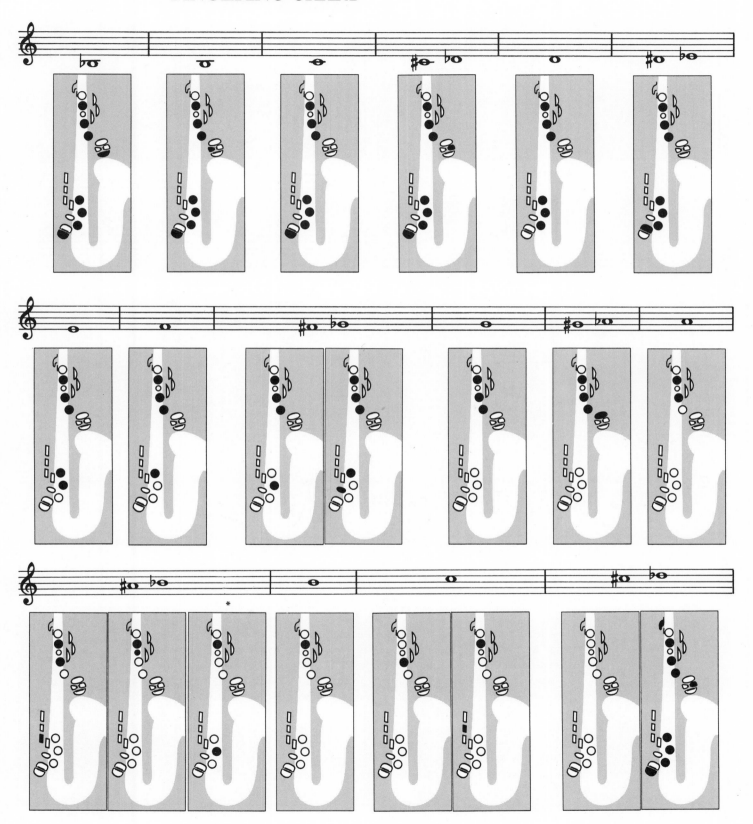

*B♭ can also be played by using the first finger R.H. instead of the second finger. This additional fingering for B♭ can also be used in the upper register by adding the octave key.

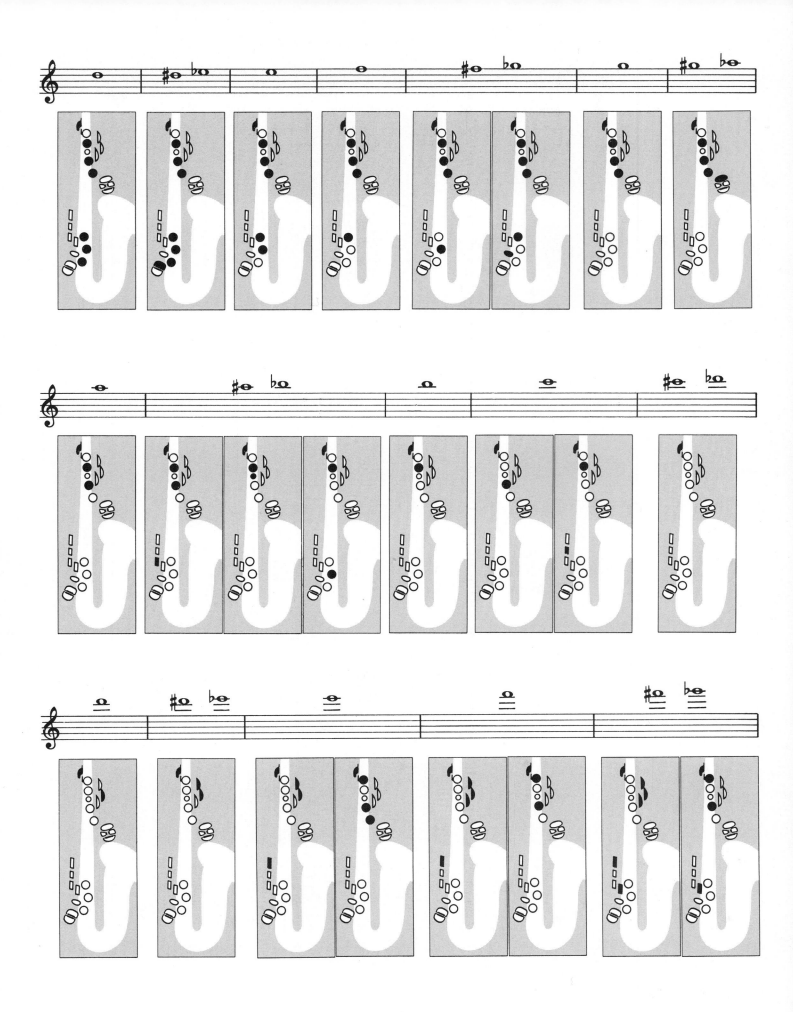

Reproduced and printed by
Halstan & Co. Ltd., Amersham, Bucks., England